D1097636

Black Fin
A Novel by
Mary Frisbee

BLACK FIN
a novel by Mary Frisbee

NORTH AMERICAN
REVIEW PRESS
Cedar Falls, Iowa

ACKNOWLEDGEMENTS

Thank you to the staff of the North American Review Press—to Shelly Criswell (Managing Editor), Grant Tracey (Fiction Editor), and supporting Staff—for this amazing publishing opportunity.

I want to thank Ken Bleile, PhD, Certificate of Clinical Competence in Speech-Language Pathology, for generously sharing his knowledge concerning mutism; and Cindy Huwe, MD for setting me straight on medical issues.

Any errors concerning these areas are entirely mine.

To Jerry Stern

an extraordinary writing teacher

NOTE FROM THE EDITORS

A red car points west. Darkness, plush pine trees, and a lemon slice of moon backlight it. A gas pump nudges the car's rear bumper. The car's gleam jumps from the screen like splashes of paint, screaming blood and passion, courage and mischief.

We can't think of a better way to define the *Gas Station Pulp Imprint* than this insignia on the back cover. A return to the past that also glances forward to the future, the west, the direction the car is pointing, and a possible new frontier in crime noir publishing. We want to travel the blue highways to the inner lives of complex psychological characters.

As fans of pulp noir, we have a respect for the past but also want to move forward into the present: retro three-chord rock with a hard bop, jazzy backbeat. We're not into parody or postmodern mockery.

This is the goal of the NAR Press's new Gas Station Pulp fiction contest, and we're proud to recognize Mary Frisbee's novel *Black Fin* as our first contest winner.

—GT & SC

Chapter One

Carved by the sea from black basalt, the walls of my cave are textured with sharp facets. At high tide, the Pacific sweeps in, leaving behind flotsam when the seawater drains back out. The seaweed and corpses of broken creatures lie abandoned for six hours until the tide returns and scrubs it all away, leaving fresh debris. I close my eyes and breathe deeply. Sea caves smell cold, tangy with iodine and salt. My favorite scent, wild and clean. This cave is my tepee, my A-frame, my cathedral. My final shelter.

I drop my pack on the sand and listen. The coast highway runs along the top of the high cliff under which this cave has formed, but no hint of engine noise can be heard, drowned out by the steady white noise of the surf. My cave doesn't have an official name nor does it appear on maps. Locals call it 'that cave in the little cove near Bridge Creek Wayside.' I've named it Wiley Cave after me, Olive Wiley. The entrance is a tall, triangular hole shaped like a shark's fin, and the south cave wall extends out to the sea, a jagged ridge curving to form a miniature bay. To reach this spot I have to walk a mile from the wayside parking lot, calculating the tides. The cave can't be accessed until the tide has gone out. If I'm caught in the cave by the incoming tide I'll drown, my body swept out on the ebb with the other detritus.

The floor of my cave drifts up and down during the year, altering with the weather and the surf. Often the cave is soaring, much of the sand washed away. Other times the sand deepens, bringing the ceiling nearer to my head. One morning when the cave was piled high, I encountered a bearded man clad only in cutoffs lying on his back, a flashlight aimed at the peaked ceiling. His pale gaze skittered across my face as a rock skips on water. In a solemn voice he informed me a clear crystal circle was embedded in the rock through which he could see into the inner world. I saw nothing, most likely because I'm not sufficiently spiritual. I stalked to my car, pissed off at the New Ager woo-wooing my personal sanctuary.

Today the cave is severely vertical, the ceiling towering above. It isn't an ideal tide—not a king tide—but it'll be big enough to do the job. What happens in the cave at high tide? I imagine the agitation of a giant washing machine set to Cold/Cold. The relentlessness of the sea fascinates me, the waves eternally seeking and cracking and eroding the cave walls. I'd like to see it in action, but I won't be awake to witness seawater assaulting the stubborn rock. I have the grit to die, but I don't plan on suffering.

Examining the leavings in the cave, I list the highlights in my beach journal: bull kelp, witch's hair, bladderwrack.

Three amber agates, one chunk of quartz, seven red jaspers. A lifeless western seagull, its handsome white and gray feathers flattened and pathetic. A piece of frosted green sea glass and a dirty white plastic bleach bottle from China with a wacky, cross-eyed cat logo. I stash a perfect sand dollar the size of a quarter in my pocket. The light has dimmed considerably when my entry is finished.

The temperature is about fifty-five degrees with a stiff northerly breeze, a typical summer evening at the coast. Wearing jeans, a long-sleeve tee, fleece vest, rain parka, ski hat, and hikers with wool socks, I'm protected from the chill. I clear rocks and seaweed from a section in the middle, pull my sleeping bag from the backpack, and spread it out. Sitting cross-legged, I eat my dinner of fresh Dungeness crab caught this morning in the bay. I went home after hauling up a legal male. Chopped him in half with the cleaver, cleaned, cooked, and picked him. After squeezing lemon over the chunks of white meat, I savor each bite. It tastes like the ocean smells. The perfect last meal.

After dinner, I pee in the back of the cave where the walls narrow into solid rock. At the sleeping bag, I remove my boots and climb in, cozy and warm. Too warm. I free my arms. Better. Makes it easier to drink from the Grey Goose bottle.

Settling comfortably onto my camp pillow, I contemplate the triangular cave entrance framing bands of sand, sea, and sky lit by a cloudy northwest sunset. The sun sinking toward the sea is obscured by layers of blue-gray haze. Ivory rays stabbing through the clouds illuminate patches of platinum on the surface of the far water. My chest aches from the beauty. The cloud strata gradually turn slate, and it grows dusky in the cave. Long milky rollers creep ever nearer the cave entrance. High tide in an hour.

I honestly don't have any deep last thoughts. I've gone through the stages—anger, sorrow, grief—and now I'm spent and in pain. The amber vial of Vicodin tucked in my inside breast pocket feels radioactive, generating its own heat source. I sip the vodka with tiny swallows so I won't throw up—my departure must go without a hitch. I conjure up Phyllis, James M. Cain's doomed character in *Double Indemnity*, and how longingly, desperately, she'd spoken of the shark, of death: "I want to see that fin. That black fin. Cutting the water in the moonlight."

A shining aqueous serpent slithers through the cave entrance, following a shallow channel through the sand. It insinuates itself around the drying seaweed and stones, soaking the seagull's feathers. I fish out the plastic vial and thumb it open. Shake out a tab. Hold it up to the fading light: a pearl of great price. Pop it in and swallow it with a sip of Grey Goose. Another. Then another. Like eating Skittles. Twenty should do it. Take it easy, one by one. The mercurial channel spreads in a sheet across the cave floor. Nowhere near me yet. When the tide reaches here, I'll be out. Another pill. Another swig.

I close my eyes as warmth closes in from the edges, erasing pain as it slides toward my core. I've dreamed of this celebration for the past two months, the joy of one Vicodin multiplied by many, made insidious by the vodka. What a delicious high! Comfort flows and my limbs relax as all care ceases. I've had tragedy and strife in my young life, but dying is the easiest thing I've ever done.

I open my eyes to witness the fading setting sun, perchance to glimpse that black fin, but where I expect to see the upside-down vee with the sea beyond, two dark figures are wading into the cave towing an inflatable dingy. I blink, uncomprehending. I can barely make out the black and white silent movie being acted out in the roar of the fast-approaching surf. Weird. Vicodin+vodka hallucination? I widen my eyes, fighting unconsciousness.

They pause, one on each side of the dingy, and upend it so that floppy bundles splash into the deepening water. The black silhouettes turn and slosh out, drawing the empty boat behind them. Twin backs with white letters: **DOUGLAS DOUGLAS**. Or maybe there's only one person and I'm seeing double.

My eyelids droop. None of my business. Sip and swallow. Almost there. But as I plant the vodka in the sand by my side, a filament of curiosity flares in the darkness. Guys in slickers. Who are they? I can't bear it if the bundles touch me. The teensy flame flashes into fury. This stupid intrusion is intolerable. A warning signal pierces my addled brain: *If you want to find out what's in the bundles, you better do it fast.*

Struggling to sit up in the confines of the sleeping bag, I fumble with the zipper and bat the ripstop away. Rolling to my side, I cram four fingers down my throat. My body resists, desiring insensibility more than life. I probe deeper and convulse a glut of vodka and pills and crabmeat onto the sand. I stick my hand in deeper. Buck out a final bunch of poison.

I grope for my pack. The zippers are so complicated. What was I looking for? The bitter rawness in my throat helps me focus. Fumbling a mini flashlight from a pocket, I hit the button and play a wavering beam around the cave. The bundles float nearer, bumping each other with the motion of the waves. I tentatively stand, get tangled in the bag, and flop to the sand, the thick twist of nylon and down unbearable against my legs. Kicking free, I attempt to rise. There seems to be something wrong with my legs and I take another pratfall.

I get it—I have to crawl. At the water's edge, I grab for the nearest bundle, miss. Grab. Miss. Catch it on the third try and drag it out of the water. It's heavy and hangs up on the rocks.

I need both hands. Think. Keep the light dry, Olive. I stick the flashlight in my mouth and bite the metal. Genius. I dig in, grasp sopping fabric, and heave. Lurch backwards on my knees, hauling the bundle. Heave again and pull it out of the surf. All of my little baked brain cells scream, protesting the bitter cold. I struggle to my feet, swaying, stocking feet gaining a bit of purchase on the wet sand. Punch-drunk, I lean forward and wade in, the icy water shocking my ankles. A wave pulses and pushes the smaller bundle toward me. It weighs less and tows more easily.

I shine the flashlight on my haul. Aw, for fucksake—the bundles are people. An adult and a child, little, age four or five. They are clothed in sopping Northwest beach attire: jeans and fleece pullovers. The child is also wearing a rain jacket and yellow rubber boots printed with red ladybugs. The adult is in stocking feet. Soaked strands of hair like seaweed stripe the white skin of their faces. I thrust my fingers to the adult's throat. Nothing. No pulse. Try the wrist. Same result. I push the soaked strands aside: a woman, with staring brown eyes and waxen blue-white skin. Utterly dead.

I flop over and test the child's carotid. A steady beat. Press my hand over the heart. Thudding slow and strong. Long dark hair, probably a girl. She breathes regularly, in and out. I gently thumb an eyelid up—her pupil is huge. Drugged? That makes two of us, kid. A freezing wave nudges my feet. I can finish the job or save the child.

Fuck.

Clutching the child to my chest, I stagger to the back of the cave and lay her on the sand. Still with the flashlight between my lips, I rip off her soaked, freezing clothing. Yep, a girl. I tuck her into the sleeping bag and zip it tight under her chin. I retrieve my pack before the Pacific snatches it.

Steeling myself to search the deceased woman's pockets, I discover a slim billfold and a set of keys. I stash them in my own jacket as a swell washes the woman's feet. Most of the mouth of the cave is now obscured with invading waves. I fight the cloying fog from my brain. Nothing I can do for her. I dig out my phone and photograph her, several views of the face and body. I'm sorry, I tell her, so sorry to leave you all alone in the dark.

At the side of the kid, I discern she's still breathing. I frantically scan the cave walls for a way to get her above the water, though I have no idea how high today's tide will rise. Is there a ledge wide enough for the child? There! Deep enough for a skinny person. Pebbles, sand, and driftwood rain over my jacket as I scoop off the rough surface of the niche and shove the bundle of clothes into the end of it. The flood is inexorable, higher now, slapping at the sleeping bag. I drag it above the surge, glimpsing the progress of the tide with the flashlight. My boots are floating and I snag them before they disappear. I fling everything toward the back and position the child under the ledge.

Her inert weight is difficult to thrust up onto the stone shelf. She rolls off twice, until with a terror-stricken heave, I pack her solidly with her stomach toward the wall, making sure her face is turned to the air. I stuff the backpack and boots in after her. The waves are licking at my feet. The roar of the surf is amplified by the cave's shape, adding to the nightmare. How the hell am I going to fit into the niche? I giggle as the absurdity of this problem hits me; a few minutes ago I was ready to off myself. Now I'm worried about surviving? Get a grip, Olive.

I desperately yearn to rest on the sand and wait for oblivion, but I envision the distress of the child if she awakens alone. What if she rolls off and falls into the water and drowns or is battered to death by the surf? Or survives only to bump into the frigid bodies of two dead women? Unthinkable to do that to a child.

The cacophony inside the cave is terrifying. Teeming, sucking noises echo against the black walls. A bullying wave rolls smoothly in, obliterating the last margin of sand in the cave, soaking my jeans. Adrenaline hits my addled system, but in spite of my panic I have the presence of mind to turn off the flashlight and stick it in my pocket. Blind, I scrabble for a toehold. I hook my fingers on the edge of the ledge, find purchase with one foot, and hang there, clinging with my fingertips and my toes. The water slaps and teases, an unseen menace coming for me in the darkness.

In sheer horror, I catapult up onto the slim margin left on the shelf, teetering on my side. I roll inward, wedging her tight, gaining a few precious inches. Another wave crashes, flinging freezing spray over my body so precariously perched on the narrow shelf. I hang on as my butt and legs grow soaked and numb. My chest is suffused with heat from the child. I wait in apprehension.

Our hours in utter blackness begin in fear but still I have to fight sleep. If I pass out, I'll roll off the ledge and drown. Then what will happen to her? I sing all the lyrics I can remember to Beatles's songs, "Back in the USSR," "A Day in the Life," ". . . Leaving the note that she hoped would say more. . ." What comes next? I start to name all the counties in Oregon, but can only recall nine. *Pi*—don't get far, 3.141. I list all the colors of green in the woods: moss, chartreuse, spruce, leaf, fern, asparagus, forest, myrtle, pine, teal. Olive. I hallucinate that the sea sloshing below is coming for me. I describe the sounds I hear in the dark: slapping, booming, swishing, lapping, gurgling, spattering, sloshing, seething. Drowning. I reconstruct the plot of *Sunset Boulevard*, envisioning the consummate noir opening shot: the body of Joe Gillis floating face down in Norma Desmond's Hollywood swimming pool. The time passes agonizingly slowly.

Finally I am certain high tide has passed and we aren't going to drown. The water will start falling soon. The slowly passing time becomes wearisome. Stay awake, Olive. The kid is motionless. I'm grateful, can't stay balanced on the edge of the narrow shelf if she struggles. I wonder what they gave her? I wonder who 'they' are, the people in the **DOUGLAS** jackets. I wonder how the woman died, and where, and why. Was she the girl's mother? My lower half is numb. My back's fairly dry. If I ever get out of here, I'll write a testimonial letter to Patagonia: *Your fabulous Gore-Tex jacket allowed me to survive a wet freezing night in a sea cave!* My hip and shoulder ache from lying on the rough rock. I cushion my head on the kid's shoulder as everything I've managed not to think about floods my mind.

I'm petite, blonde, and cute, twenty-seven years of age. Everybody likes Olive Wiley. Why not? I'm smart and amiable, remember coworkers' hobbies, what they like to read, their spouses' names. The teachers ask for Olive when they have tech issues.

They shouldn't. Much better for them to request Nathan or John, the other IT staff for the school district. Typical nerds: contemptuous of their clients, irritated by the demands of a stupid job, soft in the bottom, and lonely in the heart. But they're honest. They're overworked and too unimaginative for a life of crime. They won't steal your secrets.

But sweet little Olive, with the old-fashioned name? I'll steal you blind and you'll never suspect me. I'll listen to your tech woes, cheerfully fix the problem, memorize your passwords, read your correspondence, and rifle your desk drawers. I have access to grades, salaries, complaints, and punishments. School documents lead to parents, thence to the other residents of my small town and their supposedly secure records. I can piece together a remark overheard at the supermarket with a local news bulletin, connect a memo from the principal's office at the high school with an item from the Chamber of Commerce site. I draw mental connections and conclusions, which if diagrammed, would be interwoven into a net of complex, color-coded lines superimposed over a map of the district. It's all in my head. My pretty blonde head.

I can talk to anyone. The trick is to match my demeanor to coworkers' moods. Superintendent's secretary upset about a death in the family? I share her pain, my blue eyes soft with sympathy. A group of teachers invites me to go out for a drink? I can tell a joke with the best of them, hold my liquor, always buy a round or two. Nobody notices they haven't really learned anything about my past or that this bubbly chick doesn't speak of family, friends, or lovers.

In my town, everybody likes Olive. While I down my espresso at the convenience store on 101 in the morning, I've caught up on the daily gossip, listening to the chatter as I browse news sites. The sheriff's deputy comes in, the one who gossips too freely?—and I learn who's been picked up for DUI. The clerk chats with the customer who buys a twelve-pack each morning, and I soon know who's fucked up a construction job. I hear whose daughter's pregnant, who's been hauled to jail for beating the shit out of his wife, who's cooking meth. I'm a person not much gets by. Information is currency.

My *Jeopardy!* categories of expertise would be 'Creatures of the Oregon Coast', followed by 'Crime Novels', 'Fucked-Up Families', 'Film Noir', 'Nefarious Things To Do On Computers', and 'The Pacific'—especially the last. I spend a lot of time alone on the beach. I'm intimate with my section of the Pacific shore: the tides and phases of the moon, streams, coves, and headlands. I enumerate sea creatures and mammals. I keep not only a diary of my beach finds, but also a bird list. I can catch and cook a meal of crabs or clams or mussels. I'm tied into the Marine Animal Rescue Resource and am acquainted with the aquarium staff members. I heard about the dead whale fifteen minutes after she'd washed up on Ona Beach and was out there five minutes later. When not on the beach, I'm home viewing films from my collection of noir DVDs.

But mid-winter, my beach rambles grew shorter, my hours spent sleeping longer. Though I never called in sick, something wasn't normal. When I started to feel even crappier, I made an appointment with my doctor. She listened carefully and got me into the stirrups for an exam. Helping me sit up, she told me there was a tennis-ball-sized mass over my left ovary. Tests would be done. I'd need to see a surgeon. The mass would be removed and biopsied.

Little abrupt there, doc. "A biopsy," I echoed.

"Look, it's most likely benign. Fortunately, most ovarian cysts aren't malignant. Let me schedule you with a surgeon. We need to know for sure."

I agreed but wasn't certain I wished to find out for sure. The sole person I'd ever loved had died of cancer. She'd suffered so—emaciated, bald, shivering, and vomiting. I would not go through it. I would not. Nothing in my sad, lonely existence was worth that kind of misery.

The day before surgery, I drove to the northernmost town in my district to assist Melissa Vandevere with the online gradebook all teachers had been required to utilize. Wending my way through the village of sagging pre-fab modules abutting aging Lewis and Clark Elementary, I came upon B-4, beyond which lay the football field with its dinky grandstand. The nearest light standard was covered with a huge messy osprey nest. I heard the youngsters beeping in the nest, and as I peered up, papa sailed in with a fish in his talons. All of this would be razed when they moved to the school being constructed up the hill out of the tsunami zone. Will the city work around the light pole and the nest? I'll have to stick my nose into the matter and ensure (by hook or by crook) the osprey nest is left undisturbed.

I navigated the deserted, battered desks of B-4 and knocked on the open door of Melissa's miniscule office. She gave me a welcoming smile. A pretty brunette in her thirties, with creamy skin and an ingenuous smile, she taught full-time while single-handedly raising three kids and taking care of her disabled mother.

"Olive! Omigod, I'm so glad to see you. Coffee?" She indicated the Mr. Coffee on the ancient typing stand at the side of her desk.

"Love some."

"You like one creamer, right?"

"Thanks! Sorry you got stuck teaching in the slums."

"It's fine." She handed me a mug emblazoned World's Best Teacher, the twin of her own. Melissa sketched a toast toward me with her mug, sighing, "I've received twenty-four of these in the last eleven years."

"You're a great teacher. You deserve more," I tell her. "Teachers should be chauffeured to school in limos."

"Aww, shucks." She lowered her eyes and smiled, pleased. "Actually? I'd rather have a Dutch Brothers gift card. How are you doing?"

"I'm great. Thanks for asking, Melissa."

"Text me next time you're up here. I'd love to grab a drink after work."

"Sounds fun!" I fixed my eyes on the computer monitor. "Okay, busy lady. What's the problem?"

"I got off on the spacing and entered the last ten grades in error? And now the program won't let me correct the grades, which is weird?"

"Let me take a look. Please enter your password."

"Oh, its fine. I trust you completely. It's pelican#1978."

I entered the password and opened the grading software. "Want to take a break? Go out and enjoy the sun."

Melissa smiled. "I guess you don't need me bugging you while you work your magic." She took a sweater from where it hung from a nail and dug her cell out of her purse. "I'll be outside."

I fixed the problem—easy peasy—and wrote out a reminder about the correct procedure. Sipping my coffee, I noted that the closet sucked. Fake-wood paneling, worn green metal desk, dented gray file cabinet. But her walls were covered with cheerful crayon drawings. A brightly-colored poster hung over the desk: 'Everyone is welcome at this school! This is a no bullying zone.'

I have access to the principal's files— Lewis and Clark is definitely not a no-bullying zone. Melissa did the best she could, spending extra time with those kids whose parents were meth dealers, who lived in crappy cars or on ramshackle boats moored in the bay, whose only meals were the breakfast and lunch served at school. Fucked-up kids who took it out on each other. They had no idea how much they needed the Melissas of the world. Maybe if mine had lived, my life of crime would have passed as a mere teen aberration.

I dug through the chaos in the belly drawer of her desk: office supplies, affirmation stickers, fruit-shaped erasers, coins, pencils. Sliding my hand to the back of the drawer, I scooped the stuff forward. Aha. An orange pill container. Vicodin, prescribed by a local dentist. Melissa must have had dental work done and forgotten the pills. I slipped the bottle into my messenger bag. Snooped the rest of the drawers, helping myself to her Hershey's kisses. Glanced into her purse. Nothing interesting.

Outside, Melissa was watching the osprey nest. She said, "The fledglings will be flying soon."

"Yep. Papa brought them lunch as I was coming in." The beepbeepbeep continued from the nest. "They're insatiable."

As we hugged goodbye, I promised her I'd be in touch. I drove south, anxious about following the pre-surgery routine before going into the hospital at 5:30 a.m. the next day.

The bad news was relayed by the surgeon, who told me he'd found cancer and done a hysterectomy, but it had spread. With chemo and radiation I'd have a chance. A small one. He'd held up his hand, forefinger and thumb a quarter inch apart. His staff set up a series of appointments with a cancer clinic in Corvallis. I hadn't kept any of them.

Chapter Two

I come back to the present by falling and landing with a solid thud on the hard-packed sand. I struggle to rise, rubbing my hip in the chill. I feel shockingly bad—nauseated, aching, my head splitting. I smell salt air, hear the shushing ocean, and find momentary comfort in discovering I am in my cave. Fumbling in my jacket I bring out the flashlight. The tide has receded.

Girl! Where is she? I shine the light onto the top of her head. I lay my hand on her back, sense her regular breathing. Shivering, I wobble across the sand, flashing the light all around. The cave is empty. No body. I slump just outside the cave. The receding waves are a few feet away. Sun's not up. Stars are poised in the deep-violet sky over the long blue surf. I'd kill for a quadruple-shot venti latte. The pain in my pelvis stabs and burns. I pull out the Vicodin and swallow a tablet. Reluctantly, as though peering through foggy dusk, memories of the night come to me.

What happened to the body of the woman once she was taken by the tide? Who was she? Mother? Babysitter?

Auntie? I'll check out the wallet when I feel up to it. At dawn I'll inspect the beach. Have to be careful, it would be traumatic for the kid to see her body.

My mind skitters around the fact that a human being has been murdered. I envision the black figures who dumped her, towing the bodies in an inflated dingy, wearing jackets with **DOUGLAS** printed in bold sans serif font. The exact jackets worn by the Douglas Fire District volunteer and staff firefighters.

I study the victim's blue face on my phone. Disquieted, I turn my phone off and pop out the battery.

I weep for the woman. For the girl. For my useless, dying body. It's hard to accept that any of the men and women of the fire department who keep our houses safe and rescue the hapless could also leave a corpse and a live child in a flooded sea cave. I can see them in the shipshape firehouse at the 4th of July fundraiser, cooking hotdogs, serving soft drinks, urging people to contribute to the fireworks collection jar. Laughing. Joking. High on the anticipation of going out on the bay to blow shit up for the entertainment of the masses.

Returning to the ledge, I shine my light up to see a pair of huge frightened eyes staring over the edge. I summon up a smile as I turn the beam toward my face.

"Hi, there. My name is Olive." Silence.

"What's your name?" Silence. Her small scratched hand emerges and touches her lips.

"Are you thirsty?" She says nothing. As I reach for the pack at her feet, she shrinks away. I back off. "I'm sorry. I need the water bottle." I wait.

Finally I dig the bottle out of the pack and she allows me to help her sip.

"Do you have to pee?" She squinches her eyes, shakes her head.

"Wet in there, huh?" I ask with sympathy. She nods.

"Shall we get you out of there?" She opens wary eyes.

"Your parents warned you about stranger danger?" She blinks.

I smile at her. "I believe this is sort of a special situation, since your folks aren't here right now. I'm the adult and you need someone to care for you. I promise I won't hurt you. I promise I'll get you home." She studies my face, nods.

I unzip the bag. Grey daylight has stolen into the cave and we can see each other now. A pause, then she holds out her arms. She wraps herself around me as I hoist her off the ledge. My throat closes and I tear up. The novelty and wonder of her small body is overwhelming.

I struggle to level my voice. "I'm going to put you down for a sec, okay?" I strip off my jacket and wrap her tightly, lift her up, and carry her out of the cave. I sit with her on my lap. She doesn't speak but I sense a hum emanating from the chest pressed close to mine. It's been a long time since I touched anybody.

I am without words. We stare out to sea as we sit together companionably. Why isn't the kid hysterical? Crying? Asking a million questions? Demanding milk and cereal?

Probably the child is still in shock and also drugged-up. What did the men use to dope her? What did she see? Does she realize her mother or babysitter is dead? Her breathing slows. She's asleep. I watch the sky gradually dawn on a whole new world.

The bright sun shines on the clothing, sleeping bag, and pack spread out on the beach to dry. The wind is up and I've used rocks to secure her clothing near where she's enclosed in my jacket. I've searched the immediate stretch of beach and haven't sighted the woman's body. I keep glancing at the surf, loath to see a dark form drifting in the waves.

Sipping from the water bottle, I examine the wallet. Her name is—was—Nichole Jeanne Atkinson, her address in Portland. I've matched the photos from her driver's license and an ID card from the Portland Art Museum to my memory of her face. She was thirty-one years old, a member of the Sierra Club and the Humane Society. Library card from Multnomah Public Library system. Credit cards. Voter registration indicates she's a Dem. Two hundred fifty-seven dollars in cash and a withdrawal slip dated three days ago from an ATM in Philomath. There's a photo of a girl sitting on the beach whose face matches the sleeping child; written on the reverse side in neat cursive: Sarah, age five. A tidy wallet. I assume Nichole was Sarah's mother. I sort through the key ring: a Toyota fob and three keys. Hearing faint music, I glance behind me.

The child stands on my jacket with her arms widespread and her face turned to the sun. She is humming a song I don't recognize. The area before the cave is protected from the wind by the rocky ridge, and I can tell the sun's rays feel warm. Still, I see fine goose bumps on her thighs. She has white areas the shape of a two-piece bathing suit on her body and the rest of her skin is golden.

I say, "Sarah?" She stares at me with grey eyes luminous in her tanned face. Her pupils are still dilated. Her hair is the color of coffee beans, wild and tangled.

"Sarah's your name?" She nods.

"Do you remember me?" Sarah stares, unalarmed. Too calm. Shock? I have no idea. I need Google. Search: *behavior of children whose mothers are murdered*.

"Can you say Olive?" A shake of the head—no.

"More water?" She hesitates. Kicking the sand a little, she nears me, takes the bottle, and gulps, spilling on her tummy. I find a tissue and wipe it off.

"Hungry?" Sarah is wary.

"Sarah, I'm not going to hurt you." A long moment. Then she plops down beside me.

"Aren't you cold?" She shakes her head no. There are those goose bumps, though, so I retrieve the jacket and wrap her up.

22

"Do you remember what happened yesterday?"

Sarah scowls, her face clouding over. I don't push her. How can she possibly have assimilated whatever had happened to her mother the night before? I will let her be until she shows an inclination to communicate.

We munch on granola bars. I know nothing about kids. Never babysat, never had siblings, never taught. Have no idea how to talk to children. My own childhood was like being raised by wolves— no help in the present situation. I have enough common sense to keep a kid warm, fed, and watered. But dealing with a half-stoned, traumatized child? No clue. She's quiet, gazing out to sea. What is she thinking about? What has she seen?

I consider my other problem. I've been reviewing the scanty knowledge I have about the volunteer firefighters in Douglas, Oregon, fifteen or so men and women. The station has two full-time staff, Jill and Martin Ponsler. They're both trained firefighters and EMTs. There's another full-time EMT, a couple of part-time professional firefighters, and the rest are volunteers. I suppose the station's well-equipped for a village: two hook and ladders, ambulance rescue units, a couple of four-wheel-drive trucks with equipment lockers, jet skis, semi-rigid inflatable boat.

I know only a few of the volunteers. I envision my skein of interlinking lines on the map. The sheriff's deputies assigned to Douglas share a station with the firefighters, so they all know each other. Manny Thorp's brother Al is a county sheriff's deputy in Newport. So is his cousin, Tiny Bigelow. Anna Spinks' aunt is an Oregon highway patrolwoman. Jill Ponsler's father Ray Mandeville is on the city council. He financed my trip to Paris last Christmas by paying me quite a bit of money anonymously, due to the miracle of electronic payments. Mandeville owns a bar, three McDonald's franchises, and has a stake in a resort hotel in Lincoln City. I'd hacked his email and dug up so much municipal malfeasance, Ray had been a piece of cake to blackmail.

So, at least three links from the fire department to law enforcement and another to a corrupt town official, as well as day-to-day familiarity between cops and firefighters. What would happen if I reported that a body had been dumped by two firefighters, probably with connections to law enforcement? Would everyone get real busy and ferret out the perpetrators in their midst? Or would there be a closing of ranks? Would I perhaps be accused of kidnapping and murder? Would Sarah be protected? And what was Nichole Atkinson's connection to the town of Douglas?

My uneasiness grows. Where to turn? The majority of the staff and volunteer firefighters are sure to be straight shooters but loyalty in such an organization is fierce. Would they protect the secrets of their cohort? Who to trust? I gaze at Sarah. Of course my instinct is to contact the law. My wish is to get her to someone in authority and get back to killing myself. And even if I wanted to take care of a kid, how much longer can I even take care of myself, let alone keep her out of danger?

Movement up the beach catches my attention. I unpack my binoculars from the backpack and focus. A green Lincoln County Sheriff's Department SUV is creeping out from the wayside onto the sand. Three surfers in sleek black wetsuits emerge from the waves and meet the deputies, gesticulating, pointing to the ocean. The SUV veers to the north as a red truck backs across the beach, steering a trailer loaded with two jet skis toward the water's edge. Another red truck follows. Multiple figures in Douglas Fire District jackets swarm around the trailer. Soon the jet skis break out into the surf.

It seems the body of Nichole Jean Atkinson has been spotted in the water.

I jostle Sarah gently and lift her to her feet. After swiftly gathering our things together, I grab her hand and we dash into the cave. Sarah squirms as I struggle to dress her, grimacing and twisting, resisting the damp gritty clothing.

I'm shocked to find I want to shake her. Hard.

I take deep breaths. "Your clothes will be a bit uncomfortable but we need to go, you understand? So let's get dressed." She shakes her head no.

I sit back and consider the activity at the wayside. Whoever ditched Sarah and her mother will be here soon. But wait. While the perpetrators knew the child had been in the vicinity, nobody else in authority would. The murderers will be finessing the situation. Do sheriff's deputies search for others as a matter of course when a corpse is brought to shore? Oh, my aching head.

Doesn't matter. The bad guys are missing a body. I have to assume the pair who hauled Nichole and Sarah into the cave will eventually scour the beach nearby. We have to be gone before that occurs. At any second I expect to see a red truck break away and streak toward us across the sand.

I realize I've made my decision.

My Subaru isn't accessible, parked at the wayside smack in the middle of all the official activity. I have Nichole Atkinson's keys but no inkling about her Toyota's whereabouts. It isn't possible to scale the cliff rising above us. We have to walk south. What the hell, let Sarah go bare. I stuff her clothes in the pack and put my arms through the straps. Pawing through the driftwood pile at the base of the bluff, I select a couple of branches.

"Are you old enough to help me?" I show her how to use a stick to scrub out our footprints. She clenches it in both fists and scratches industriously. We sweep backward to the water until the wavelets wash our feet. Our handiwork's not convincing, appears exactly as though someone has tried to disguise footprints with scrapes and gouges. But it's the lesser of two evils—at least our specific, identifiable prints are obliterated. I take a final look with the binoculars at the action on the beach: same vehicles in the same positions. The jet skis have paused, bobbing beyond the breaking surf.

I hold out my hand. "Now we're going to run."

We trot through the shallows around the jutting outcrop of rock forming the cove at Wiley Cave. On the other side, a wide beach extends south into the far distance. I draw a relieved breath now we're out of sight. There's no one else visible on this stretch, not such a miracle on the coast. Often you don't see a soul for miles.

We drop our sticks in the surf and Sarah skips ahead, oblivious to the chill. She lets the freezing, lacy waves slide up her bare feet. I scan the forest that stops abruptly at the edge of the cliff. It's all national forest land along here, undeveloped. The whole Oregon coast is public property, unless it's military. We can't trespass on private property going to and from the beach, but once we're on the sand, it's all ours. It's about three miles to the next state park wayside. Is there an empty private house in which we can shelter before then? We're a bit south of my stomping grounds, so I'm not quite as familiar with the territory. We have to keep moving.

I empathize with the difficulties Sarah must be having this morning, about how she doesn't speak and her emotionless behavior. It's idiotic I haven't talked to her, treating her as though she is both mute and deaf. She hears just fine. I need to use my voice to make a connection. I ruefully remember how scared I'd been most of my childhood, how nobody had bothered to consider my feelings or talk with me, until I'd been rescued by my librarian. I should be better than this.

"Can you say my name?" I ask her. Sarah shakes her head no.

"It's Olive, right? Listen, would you mind holding my hand?" She fits her icy fingers into mine. We slosh through the shallow waves.

"What would you like to do today?" Sarah shrugs.

"Find your mommy and daddy?" She glances up at this, eyes glinting through her wind-blown hair. Sarah nods yes.

"I'll bet you're ready for lunch." She nods with emphasis.

I babble as we walk, telling her about the sea, the names of birds and the creatures in the tide pools. She doesn't answer but I can tell she's listening. In a half hour or so I spot a building glinting in the trees up above. As we grow nearer, I see there is a colony of five cottages strung out along the top of the sandstone bluff. A weathered gray staircase clings to the sheer cliff.

Sarah points to the stairs.

"Should we go up?" Sarah nods vigorously. She has a whole vocabulary of eloquent nods and shrugs.

I consider the one-level gray-green house at the top, a modest Seventies cottage with picture windows facing the sea over a wood deck. The drapes are pulled shut. I see no towels hanging from the railing. No sign of activity. We need to get off this exposed beach. I decide to chance it. Once we start up the stairs, we'll be trespassing but if anyone's home, I'll bluff. Though it might be difficult explaining why my child is naked.

At the bottom of the stairs, pain bites my gut, forcing me to bend over. I clutch the stair railing, groping for the

Vicodin. I swallow a tab. Sarah watches attentively. I dig in my pocket for a plastic box of Tic Tacs.

I show her the orange Vicodin bottle and make a fierce face. "Extremely bad for kids." She smiles. I give her the Tic Tacs and say with a loopy grin: "Appropriate for kids. Got it?" Sarah carefully pries up the tab. She shakes one out, pops it in her mouth, and returns the box.

We slowly climb up the splintering stairs. I keep an eye out for people, both on the beach below and the bluff above. I clear the top and study the place. Scruffy grass surrounds the home. A weed-choked gravel driveway leads up to a garage. No vehicles in sight. No bikes or wheelbarrows or crab traps or buckets. I deduce this is a vacation home. I saunter casually across the yard, Sarah in tow. Through the Douglas fir, I glimpse the next cottage in the row. When we gain the narrow deck, we are out of sight.

I peek through the uncurtained window into a shadowed hallway. At the end sits a table and chairs silhouetted against window light. I turn the door handle—locked. I knock and call out. No answer. I rummage in the stoneware jar full of ferns on the porch, tip it up and peer beneath—no key. Sarah wanders along the wooden deck, staring fixedly up into the eaves. I join her and see a key hanging from a nail on the side of a beam end. How'd she know?

"Wow, good eye." Sarah smiles. I have the feeling she's used to positive affirmation. I stoop and peer into her eyes. I'm relieved her pupils are almost normal-sized now.

I unlock the door and push it open. Listen. Sniff. Damp and mildew. All is quiet and dim. We move through the hallway hung with jackets on hooks and boots lined up along the baseboard. In the kitchen, the fridge is empty and clean, the sink and counters uncluttered.

"Hello?" I wait. It's quiet.

I sweep through the house, searching for occupants. No one there. At the window in the living room, I glance through the drapes at the empty beach below. This house is one of the first places I'd scout if I was a murderer and had any suspicion the kid had survived. Of course, I'd hunt north, too. Logically Sarah's body should have been near Nichole's, right? But nothing to do with the action of dead creatures in the sea follows any logic.

The killers would have their attention focused on the owner of the Subaru left all night in the wayside parking lot. They had secured Nichole's ID in a zipped pocket before dumping her body, so I should have left her wallet and keys in her fleece. When it's revealed her ID is missing, they'll know someone has been in contact with the body. They have no way of knowing if Sarah is alive. Sarah may have witnessed whatever happened before she had been drugged. Maybe she could identify the killers. But why was she left alive? Squeamishness about offing a child? Easier to leave her to drown in the sea cave? I assume the killers had set the scene so that it would be assumed that Nichole had been careless, trapping herself and her child in a cave at high tide. A clueless tourist accident.

Sarah has climbed up on the overstuffed denim couch, wrapped herself in a blanket, and burrowed into a pile of throw pillows. She can't or won't talk but she's telling me she's cold. I need to ward off a chill. I move toward the sofa, thinking I will gather her up and keep her warm with my body. But something inside prevents me. I turn aside.

In the kitchen, I turn the faucet and the water runs. I explore the laundry room off the kitchen, discover the hot water heater, study the dial, and turn it on.

"I'll draw you a bath in awhile," I call to Sarah, then jump—she's right there, trailing her blanket. She studies the shelves in the pantry, choosing a can with a picture of alphabet soup in a bowl on the label.

I dig out a saucepan from a nearby cupboard and put the soup on the stove to heat. I wrap Sarah up in the blanket and leave her at the kitchen table with a packet of crackers as I explore more thoroughly. The living and dining room flow out of the kitchen. Opening off the hallway are three dim bedrooms and two baths. The cottage is furnished with well-worn furniture, cluttered with shells and driftwood, books, toys, cushions, and magazines. It has a pleasant, lived-in feel. There's no TV, no computer. I pause to examine a shelf of framed photos. A couple—man and woman—with two boys, the same people aging through the snapshots. A nice family.

An ancient turquoise phone hangs on the kitchen wall. Might come in handy since I'm without a working cell phone. What with having to deal with a corpse in the surf, the sheriff's department has traced me by now through my car's license plate. They've accessed my driver's license, have my employment and contacts. They'll urgently want to question me. They'll see from my license info that Olive Wiley is not the victim; Nichole was brunette, had brown eyes, and stood four inches taller.

I inspect the closets. Borrow a plaid flannel robe and a smaller pink fleece. In the drawers, I find thick socks. I'm comfortable, in my element. This is what I do, poke through people's stuff. I pay particular attention to the parents' dressers, even checking the bottom of drawers for taped envelopes, but don't come across any hidden money. Another worry. We have little cash and shouldn't use my ATM or credit cards, nor Nichole's. I could track somebody through his or her plastic so I assume the sheriff's department can too.

I retrieve Sarah's wet clothes, strip off my own, throw them in the washing machine with the sleeping bag, and start it chugging. We don the robes and I sit Sarah on a kitchen chair to pull socks on her chilly feet. I set a bowl of soup before her.

"It's pretty hot. Careful sips." She dips her spoon into the soup, brings up a miniscule amount, touches it to her lips. In the pantry, I discover a bottle of grape juice and pour her a glass. She gulps noisily. Damn, I must keep her better hydrated. I'm not hungry but ladle out some soup. I sip the juice. Sarah plays with the pasta letters in her soup, moving them from side to side. I experience a brief sense of deja vu, a memory that this scene was repeated in my childhood, very

32

early on, before my parents went off the rails. Can I remember my mother laughing at a nonsense word I'd spelled out in my soup? Not sure. But I do recall that when I was about eight, I'd spilled soup on the table and my daddy, livid, had thrust my hand into the hot liquid in my bowl.

Sarah taps her bowl for attention—she's has three letters in a row: S A R. I push my bowl across to her and she spoons up the noodles and transfers them to her bowl. Soon it reads S A R A H.

"You are a smart cookie." We finish our lunch and I lead her into the bathroom.

Sarah splashes in the tub full of bubbles, playing with a squishy rubber shark. I shampoo her hair and dash to the laundry room to transfer our clean clothes to the dryer. I sit on the toilet and read aloud from an old Nancy Drew novel, *The Secret of Mirror Bay.*

Hearing a wee mew, I glance up to see her face crumple as she clutches the toy shark to her chest. A long wail comes from her open pink mouth, a sound of such pitiable woe that my heart stutters. She sobs full tilt, hard and gut-wrenching, and wildly flings the shark across the bathroom. She is frozen in the tub, her soaked hair flowing over her scrunched-up eyes, arms thrust up, fists clenched. Grabbing a bath towel, I wrap her up as I lift her from the tub. She fights me, screaming, legs kicking and arms flailing. I fold around her as she strains away, rigid. She runs out of air, sucks in a deep breath, and screams again. I croon soothingly and she crumples into me, her wailing terrible to hear. Tears are streaming down my own face. How can I comfort such pain? I carry her into the nearest bedroom and crawl under the quilt, embracing her. Her sobs gradually calm as I whisper nonsense in her ear. She gives a final hiccup and is asleep. Exhausted, I doze off, too.

I wake to thundering on the door, a deep male voice calling, "Hello? Anybody home?" More pounding, even louder. It's terrifying, like it's in the room with us. "Hey! Anybody there?" Struggling, I recall that the kitchen entrance is situated by our narrow bedroom window. Suddenly I'm wide awake.

Sarah's eyes, huge and frightened, meet mine. "Ssh," I whisper. "Be still."

Heavy footsteps cross the deck. I scooch up to peep through the gap between the curtains hanging over the bed. I can see the front end of a red truck mounted with a winch, the rest of it cut off by the garage. A tall man in jeans, rubber boots, and a jacket with **DOUGLAS** on the back, strides away from us along the deck. Wide shoulders, muscular legs, a confident stride. He wears a ball cap, dark hair curling into his collar. He turns and I glimpse his tanned, clean-cut face before I duck out of sight. I don't recognize him. He rattles the doorknob, raps on the glass; he can see clearly into the kitchen and I can't remember if I left the light on. Are our bowls sitting on the table? I hear a dull thud and a tinkle as glass falls onto the entryway floor. I panic—where can I hide Sarah?

"Excuse me, but can I help you?" A faint female voice, coming from the direction of the drive.

The man answers, friendly and easy-going. "Oh, hey. How are you? You the neighbor?" I imagine him blocking the woman's sight of the broken window with his body.

"Yeah, I am. Is there a fire? Something wrong with the Christiansen house? I've got them right here on speed dial . . ."

"No, no," the man protests. "I'm from the Douglas Fire District. We had a fatality at Bridge Creek Wayside and we suspect there may have been more than one person out there." Say your name say your name say your name, I silently chant. "Found a suspicious car in the lot. We're checking out the houses in this area."

"That's three miles from here." Her voice is skeptical. "I don't see why you're bothering us about it. I haven't seen a soul. In any case, the Christiansens aren't here. I'll call them." Good for you, lady, stick to your guns. Ask for ID.

"Absolutely not necessary if you haven't seen an intruder." His reassuring voice fades as his boots crunch on the gravel. "I gotta get back to the accident site. Sorry to trouble you, ma'am."

A deafening diesel engine revs up and there's the sound of wheels rolling on gravel. He'd said 'accident site.' So that's what they're labeling it? An autopsy would be ordered. What would the results show? What method had been used to kill Nichole?

A pause and I hear more footsteps, the neighbor's voice fading. "Ilsa, there was a fireman here. Something about . . ." She's gone.

Sarah and I lay together, hearts beating hard. She wriggles. I'm clutching her and she can't breathe. I'm stiff with fear, have to force myself to relax and smile. We're cozy in our damp nest of towel and comforter. Her hair is tangled.

"I'm going to find a hairbrush." I rise and pad down the hall.

And freeze. The kitchen light is on. Our soup bowls and glasses and the crackers sit on the kitchen table, in full view. A fitful breeze blows through the broken windowpane. The fireman knew we were here. He had deliberately split so we wouldn't be detected with a witness present. That couldn't be legit. Besides, wouldn't it be the job of the sheriff's department to canvas the neighborhood, not firemen? And cops wouldn't break in. When a body is pulled out of the sea, the coroner is called out. Evidence techs and traffic control officers—perhaps the sheriff herself—show up. Nope, no way the fireman had been on official business.

The motherfucker would be back.

Stepping gingerly over the broken glass, I peer out. No one. I open the door and listen. The neighbor is gone. I consider the garage, the only part of the home I haven't explored. There's a key rack shaped like a fish by the door. Fingering the various rings, I find a Honda key fob and another key helpfully marked "Garage." Flitting barefoot to the garage side door, I unlock it and peer in at the older model silver Honda Accord parked inside. I tiptoe across the frigid concrete and get in. The vinyl is cold through the thin flannel covering my thighs. I crank it up. The engine hiccups, stutters, and starts. A little rough but it runs. Thank you, thank you. In the glove compartment is a plastic envelope containing registration and an insurance card in the name of Ilsa Christiansen. Can the neighbor hear the engine? I shut the Honda off.

Inside I pause by the phone. Should I call someone? Who? I've already ruled out the Lincoln County sheriff's office. It's not advisable to travel north into the area where Nichole had been pulled from the sea. We could wend our way through the maze of national forest gravel roads to the east, but I don't have a map and it would be unwise to power up my phone to access one. Best to go south down the Coast Highway. The nearest sheriff's office is in Lane County, thirty miles away in Florence; there isn't a town or even a gas station before then. I imagine explaining the events that have transpired—as well as my suspicions—to a dispatcher. I imagine the futility of such a conversation. Hell. I can contact law enforcement when we get to Florence. First, do no harm. Occasionally benign neglect is the best policy.

I brush Sarah's hair and braid it, albeit unevenly. She enjoys this, closing her eyes, humming. Did Nichole go through this ritual every morning? I fetch our clothes from the dryer and we dress in our toasty jeans and tees, put on our damp boots. I make the bed and smooth the covers.

Hang up the robes—we're wearing the warm socks. Stuff a couple of unopened toothbrushes and a tube of toothpaste in my pocket. Open the medicine cabinet and grab a bottle of children's Tylenol, revealing an orange bottle. Oxycontin. Does everyone in America have narcotics in their possession? I filch both of them.

Sarah emerges from the other bedroom clutching a cardboard carton. She shows me the plastic toys and junk inside: a pirate ship, a cottage, an ambulance, a bunch of squat little figures, little green Army guys, Day-Glo plastic Easter eggs, bits and pieces of crayon. What the hell, let her have the box. I add Nancy Drew, the can opener, cans of soup, and crackers.

I leave the kitchen light on and the cluttered table exactly the way it was, switch the hot water heater off. Fireman X won't have a clue when we left or whether or not we had been in the house when he knocked. Always sow disinformation when you can. I grab the pack and lift Sarah over the broken glass. Inside the garage, she scrambles into the back seat of the Honda while I load our things. I try to buckle her in with the seat belt but she crawls over to the other side.

"What?" Sarah cups her hands at her sides, pulls an imaginary something across her chest. I get it—she's supposed to have a child seat. Shit.

I raise the trunk to reveal blankets, a battered red toolbox, and jack. Next to a giant half-empty jar of Red

Vines sits a steel lockbox, the word Beretta scrolled in gold on the lid. Huh. I tug on a Rogue Brewery ball cap emblazoned Dead Guy, their signature ale. It suits my sense of humor to wear it. No child seat. I scan the shelves of garage junk—nope.

I shut the trunk, pausing to count to ten. Leaning in the back door, I smile as the seconds tick away. "Sarah. Cookie. We have to buy a seat, okay? I'll drive very, very carefully. You'll be fine for now." Dubious, she clouds up again. Please. No screaming.

"I know your mommy would approve as long as we stop and buy a car seat soon." Reluctantly, Sarah nods, but she's unhappy. I surmise her mother has always fastened her in properly. This is the new norm. I'd never had a child seat, so how was I to know?

I kiss her on the forehead. "Thanks, Sarah." I fasten her seat belt.

I open the garage door, dancing with jitters. Start up the car and back it out. Congratulations, Olive—grand theft auto. I shut the garage door, lock the side door, hang the garage key on the fish rack, lock the kitchen door. Dash back to the Honda. I hit the gas and reverse up the driveway, careening toward 101. Sarah lets out a nervous squeal, letting me know I am *not* driving carefully.

Time to flee.

Chapter Three

The Honda hugs the tight curves of Highway 101. Towering wooded cliffs rise up on our left, plummeting to our right to the surf below. Cape Creek and the Heceta Head Lighthouse are a few miles ahead. I concentrate on the road and stay at the speed limit, drawing no attention. Firefighter X will return, requestion the neighbor, and find out about the Honda that had been parked in the garage. How long will the Honda's license plates be safe before I'm picked up for driving a stolen car? Oh, and kidnapping, of course. Paranoia's good. Paranoia will keep Sarah unharmed until I can scare up her dad or other relatives.

I glance at her in the rearview mirror, see her playing with the plastic dolls. I need to change plates. I'm driving one of the most ubiquitous vehicles on the road, but still I must replace these license plates. I consider the parking lot at Heceta Head. Lots of vehicles to choose from at the most popular feature on this stretch of the coast. But there will be too many tourists at the beloved cove on a nice summer day. Spotting the sign for the gravel parking area for the Cummins Creek trailhead, I pull in. There are seven cars there, a few people in sight preparing to hike up the trail.

As I open Sarah's door, I hear an outraged female voice: "Excuse me, but you can't travel with a child that young strapped in a seatbelt!" Shit.

Sarah glances at me like, *I told you so.*

I back out, smiling. "I know, right? Somebody broke into our car up in Yachats and stole our child seat and cooler. Can you believe it?" I'm facing a thirtyish woman, chic haircut, slim, dressed in dark, sophisticated wilderness wear. She's accompanied by a boy and girl, and they're all frowning at me as though they'd caught me beating my child in Walmart.

"Good Lord, you can't *travel*, then."

"What would you have me do, ma'am?" I spread my hands wide and make a little sorry face. That *ma'am* will burn her ass. "Nowhere to buy one between Yachats and Florence."

"You need to call somebody to bring you one," she insists. Stay calm—mustn't be memorable.

"If anyone was available, I would," I say seriously, staring directly into her eyes. "But there isn't, so we are going to drive slowly and safely to Florence, go directly to Fred Meyer, and buy a car seat. But thanks for your concern, I appreciate it."

Dismissing her with a brilliant smile, I lead Sarah toward the Porta Potty, leaving Supermom no option but to back off, fuming. I glance over my shoulder—they're donning daypacks at the rear of their SUV. Supermom is motionless, studying the Honda. After a moment, she joins her kids as they hike up the trail.

I toy with the idea of stealing both her plates and her child seat. Recognize it's a bad idea. Returning to the Honda, I pop the trunk, find a screwdriver in the toolbox. Give Sarah a Red Vine from the jar. She sucks on it as we walk past the row of cars. At the end is a battered blue Explorer. It's dusty, rusty, and filled with fast-food trash. If the owners are careless types, they won't notice their plates are all wrong. I kneel and quickly unscrew the Oregon plates, move to the front and do the same, tucking the bolts in my jeans pocket. I stay alert as we double back to the Honda. Nobody in sight. I switch out the plates and we traverse the parking lot once again. Sarah gazes up at me, puzzled.

"Fun, huh?" Sarah knits her brows. I attach the Honda's plates to the Explorer. As we stroll to our car, two middle-aged men holding hands emerge from the trees and smile at us as they stride toward a pickup truck. I strap Sarah in, hoping I won't hear a child seat lecture from the couple, and we continue south.

The Florence Fred Meyer is packed, shoppers barging along wide aisles stacked with food, drink, sporting goods, furniture, and a dizzying array of child car seats. I need to charge my phone and access *Consumer Reports* but have to be content with reading the hard copy on the boxes. I choose one suited to a child of Sarah's age and approximate weight and load it into the cart.

I trawl the aisles, spot my halibut: a woman in expensive clothing with high-priced hair glaring at a label on a bottle in the wine aisle. She has a red Birkin bag in her cart. Really, lady? You bring an Hermès handbag to buy wine at Fred Meyer? Or maybe it's a fake Birkin. I don't know. I only know it's especially delightful robbing the rich. The bag is fastened shut. I peruse the wine bottles, waiting. Ms. Birkin Bag lets out a sigh of exasperation and opens the bag, rummaging inside. She withdraws a paper and stares at it, holding it at arm's length. She makes another of the sounds, dives back in, and comes up with a glasses case. She dons a pair of readers. Drops the case in the bag, leaves the opening gaping.

As she compares the paper to the wine label, I mention conversationally to Sarah, "Don't suppose you know anything about California pinot noirs, huh?" She smiles. I push our cart forward and as we pass I ask, "Macaroni and cheese for supper?" Sarah lights up at this idea and claps her hands.

By the time we are past her, the woman's wallet is in my parka pocket.

We have checked into a mom 'n' pop motel located on the commercial highway strip of Florence and are eating mac 'n' cheese and sliced apples and drinking juice. Our room is worn and clean, with a kitchenette and a counter with two stools. Sarah is a tidy eater, spooning up a couple of pieces of pasta at a time, chewing them thoroughly. Later we'll eat the chocolate cookies Sarah chose for dessert.

I've scored three thousand bucks in cash, less than the wallet itself is worth. Out of this, I've paid for our purchases at Fred Meyer, the motel, and a tank of gas. (I'm certain Ms. Birkin Bag has already reported her credit cards stolen.) I've never known anyone outside of Vegas who carries this kind of cash. Interesting. My talents have been wasted in Douglas, Oregon.

We're secure for the night. The room is paid for in cash with a fake name on the motel registration: we are now Jennifer and Nathan Oldenburger. I had left Sarah in her new car seat, her jacket hood pulled up over her hair while I checked in at the office. I could see her through the window, as could the old guy at the counter who had peered out at the Honda. It's impossible for him to tell that she is a girl.

After dinner, Sarah dumps her box of toys on the floor. Curious, I examine the pirate ship. It's made from sturdy plastic, stamped Playmobil on the bottom. The ambulance, the bungalow—all Playmobil. These are very cool toys. The Christiansens will probably miss them. Sarah studies the stumpy figures wearing clever, painted costumes. She sets the pirates aside with the ship. She places mom, dad, and children with the house. This leaves the ambulance. The 'victim' lying on its plastic gurney and the pair of EMTs are laid by the vehicle. She pats her thighs with satisfaction: there, all sorted out.

The door locked and the chain in place, I tell Sarah I need a shower. She ignores me, absorbed in her activity. I rip the tags off the jeans, tee, socks, and underwear I'd purchased at Freddy's. Hopping in the shower, I luxuriate in the stinging stream of hot water. After drying off, I check on Sarah, who is humming softly and moving the toys here and there. I dress quickly.

I turn on the TV, mute it, and select closed-captioning. The Portland news begins. The body found on the Oregon coast is third in the broadcast. Tiffany Wade, dressed in a red Columbia parka, reports from the Bridge Creek Wayside. I'll be damned—there's my Subaru behind her, ringed with yellow police line tape.

Her lips move. The captioning with its unintentionally hilarious misspellings runs across the bottom: "Two early morning smurfers made a grizzly discovery here at Bridge Creek Wayside when they spotted the body of a woman floating in the waves. Lincoln County Sheriff's deputies were on the scene twenty minutes later, along with members of the Douglas Fire District rescue squad. Using jet skies, the body was recovered. Sheriff's officers state there was no identification on the body. The only vehicle in the parking lot was identified as belonging to a Douglas resident, Olive Kathryn Wiley. However, the driver's license photograph of Wiley does not match the victim. The sheriff's department is seeking Wiley's whereabouts as well as requesting the public's assistance in identifying the victim, who is described as about thirty years of age, with dark hare and brown eyes."

The reporter smiles into the camera, swivels to her right. "We have with us Beau Cassidy of the Douglas Fire District to describe the recovery."

And who should enter the screen but Firefighter X, the big dark-haired guy who had searched for us at the beach house. Electrified, I choke the urge to cry out. No need to alarm Sarah.

Cassidy looms over the petite reporter. The captioning runs late, never synced with his lips, making everything even more off-kilter. "Um, so, we were called out at 6:10 a.m. by the sheriff's department to investigate a report of a body in the water. We spoke to the smurfers who had spotted the victim in the water and deployed two jet skies. The body was near where the smurfers had last seen it—her. We secured the deceased and brought her to shore. After the Coroner's examination, the victim was transported to Newport." His voice is a strong baritone, his words assured.

Cassidy is good-looking, with light eyes, gray or blue, shadowed by the same DFD ball cap he'd worn when last I'd seen him. Age about the same as mine, I reckon. His demeanor is serious and confident. As he speaks, Tiffany smiles up at him, rapt. He's a fireman groupie's wet dream come true.

Should Sarah be seeing this? Hell, it's too late, she's already by my side, staring at the screen with thumb in mouth. Her body is tense—ready to scream?

I cuddle her. "Sarah, do you know that man?" She frowns and nods her head yes. A commercial begins. I turn off the TV.

"Was the man a friend of your mother's?" I ask gently. Sarah shakes her head violently back and forth—an emphatic no.

"Did she know him?" She looks unsure. Is the distinction between *friend* and *know* confusing her?

She squirms to get free from my arms and drops to her knees, attention back on her toys. I stretch out on the bed. Why doesn't she speak? Is it permanent or trauma-related? Sarah picks out the mother from the toy house and moves it near the ambulance. She removes the victim from the gurney.

I observe, riveted.

Sarah walks the little EMT figures to the gurney, carrying the mother between them, and moves the group to the back of the ambulance. They put the mother figure on the gurney and Sarah pushes it inside. She picks out the girl-child from the house as well. Sandwiching the doll between the little figures, she clumsily moves the group across the worn carpeting to the open rear door of the ambulance and manipulates the EMTs to shove the child inside. One figure goes into the back with the child. She shuts the door and tucks the other EMT into the driver's seat of the cab.

A soft purr comes from Sarah's throat, "Rrr, rrr." She pushes the ambulance rapidly across the floor and abandons it beneath the stools. Jumping to her feet, she reaches for the cookies. Time for dessert.

Tucked in bed in her flannel jammies, Sarah watches *Word Girl* on PBS while drawing with the crayons on one of the plastic eggs from her toy box. She seems to be drawing loops and dots, using all the colors she has. She looks up at me, proffering the egg. She nods at it. I take it from her hand. "It's beautiful, Sarah. Thanks."

She watches me a moment and then turns back to her show. Her face is mobile and intelligent as she follows the story; she claps and laughs at appropriate moments. Seems smart and observant. I'm glad to see her engaged, her mind off her trauma.

I toss the egg lightly in my hand. Sarah had recognized Beau Cassidy—that much was clear. Her manipulation of the toys may have indicated that she and her mother had been taken by two EMTs and forced into an ambulance. Can I trust her actions as a way of communicating a true story or is it merely imaginative play? She hadn't had the mother captured by pirates and put aboard the *Cursed Sea Dog*, so perhaps the ambulance is significant.

Was Beau Cassidy one of the EMTs in her story? Sarah's toy charade was over when the child-doll was placed into the ambulance, so perhaps Sarah's memory ended there. I knew Sarah had been drugged and most likely it had been administered inside the vehicle, if Sarah's actions were to be believed. Her memory would have been a blank until she woke up in the cave with a total stranger. I could only conjecture on what had happened in between. But Sarah must be in danger as a witness to the kidnapping and perhaps her mother's murder. Otherwise, why would Cassidy be bothering to hunt for her? For us?

I turn on my brand new tablet, connect to the motel Wi-Fi, create a fake Gmail account, and search the Oregon news sites. They reprise the facts I've already learned. The body of the woman found in the surf has still not been identified. It's odd that no one has reported Nichole missing, to say nothing of the child. Doesn't Sarah have a father? Grandparents? Cousins? There is no mention of a missing child on the websites.

I try to follow the thinking of the murderers: a car belonging to Olive Wiley is located near where they had deserted Nichole and her daughter. There is no word from Olive Wiley in response to the newscast. Neither Olive's body nor the child's have washed up on any of the nearby beaches. Nichole's body, left with full ID, now has no ID.

By now Cassidy must have returned to the beach house on the bluff to ascertain a car had been stolen. It's not much of a stretch to connect Olive and the child together.

I google Beau Cassidy. There are a surprising number of citations, but most are not the Cassidy I'm seeking. About twenty results down, I come to the Douglas Volunteer Fire District where he is listed with the others in a group photo shot outside the firehouse. He's in the second row, third from the left, grinning and large. A normal-looking, attractive guy. I peer at the other firefighters: who could be his accomplice? I remember that the figures I'd seen in the cave had been about the same height, tall. Looking at the photo, I see that the women volunteers are of medium height. So—probably Beau and another man.

I find no other references to this particular Beau Cassidy.

Why had Nichole been murdered? I google her name but Sarah shakes my foot, holding out her book. She climbs up on the bed and tucks herself under my arm. I am amazed at how good this makes me feel—I can feel a huge grin on my face. We continue reading about Nancy Drew, teen detective. Sarah's eyes droop and eventually I join her in sleep, curled up together.

In the morning, Sarah and I are in a standoff. I'm clutching a pair of scissors in one hand and my tablet in the other.

Sarah is planted defiantly on the opposite side of the bed. I have dyed my blonde locks a dark chocolate. I catch a glimpse in the mirror and barely recognize myself—I've always been a towhead. Now we need to disguise Sarah, but she's not having it.

"Sweetie, I'm sorry, but we need to cut your hair." She shakes her head violently from side to side, long locks flying, stubborn chin pointed up at me. I refuse to hold the threat of Cassidy detecting us over her, I will not use Beau-as-boogey man to scare her into submission. I'd felt so much fear as a child that it would be impossible for me to threaten Sarah in any way. I'll find another path.

What do kids want, Olive? To have carefree fun. To eat sugar. To be hugged by their mothers. Two out of three ain't bad.

I drop the scissors on the bedside table and change the subject. "What should we do today?" Her eyes are wary.

Sitting on the edge of the bed, I skim the guide to the Florence area I had picked up in the motel office.

"We could take a whale-watching trip," I propose. "Wouldn't that be fun?" Sarah shakes her head no.

I toss the brochure aside. "Or we could rent a movie. *Frozen*? I saw it in the office. We can eat Red Vines and watch it together." Sarah is motionless.

"*Frozen*?" She nods.

"Okay, then, we will get *Frozen*, but Sarah? We have to change your appearance. We can't have anyone recognize you before we can find your parents." Her hands grasp the strands of hair on either side of her face as her eyes fill with tears.

"I suppose your daddy likes your long hair." I gingerly lay down on my tummy and wrap my arms around her as she stands stiffly between the bed and the wall.

"Are you afraid your daddy won't recognize you if we cut your hair?" She nods with certainty.

I roll to my side, laughing. "Your daddy would recognize you if you had purple skin and a red mohawk. Daddies always know their little girls." What a crock.

"So let's give you a beautiful new do." After a pause, she moves out from behind the bed.

Referring to my tablet, I cut her hair short like a boy's. I comb and snip as she stands on a bath towel. I've decided not to change the color as the internet says the chemicals are not healthy for kids. Instead, I'm changing her gender and to this end, I bought boys' clothes and sneakers for her in neutral colors. No pink. But I couldn't bear to dress her in tighty-whities so I let her pick out her own panties and jammies. She skipped the Disney princesses and chose Dora the Explorer pj's: I suppose this says something about her mother.

I wince, picturing Nichole lying on a slab in the morgue with a huge Y incision splitting her torso.

Finishing up, I position Sarah in front of the mirror. Her eyes widen. She sees a whole new kid—the quintessential

English schoolboy. I hover beside her, fascinated at my own transformation. I've used a lot of makeup, surrounded my eyes with liner, brightened my mouth with red—Anne Hathaway. Sarah giggles, claps her hands. She likes it! She touches my lips, then her own. I fetch lip balm from the pack, smooth it on her mouth.

As we walk hand-in-hand to the office, I'm brought up short. What if the same clerk is on duty? I look unlike the person who checked in. Then I think, so what? Women change the color of their hair all the time. But instead of the white-haired man—'pop'—of the night before, a white-haired older woman—'mom?'—hunches over a computer.

"May we rent *Frozen*? For Room 11?"

"Sure, hon." The clerk doesn't look up from her keyboarding. "On the rack. I'll add it to your bill." I lift Sarah up and she unerringly grabs the DVD from the array on the rack. I gaze longingly at the copy of *The Big Sleep* just above.

"Thanks. I'll bring it back soon." Mom waves us off.

As we enter our room, I catch sight of the white-haired man at the end of the walkway, sprinkling plants with a hose. Inside, I settle Sarah on a pile of pillows before the TV and crank up the DVD player. She'll be occupied for a couple of hours. When it's done, we'll play on the beach.

It's an interesting thing, a reprieve from death. There's no pressure to explain anything, no desire to contact anyone, no urgency to visit my condo or pick up the mail. I couldn't care less about losing my Subaru. When you plan to off yourself, trivial stuff like mail and bills don't matter anymore. I've left a will in my apartment leaving almost everything to Melissa Vandevere—a person who's actually valuable to society deserves my ill-gotten gains. The local library will receive my extensive collection of crime novels and DVDs, as well as a sum of cash. I wrote a suicide note to tidy things up for the authorities. A note to my doctor. I'd shredded my papers, unsubscribed from online accounts, and destroyed my computer hard drive. No more secrets threaten the inhabitants of my town. Lucky them.

Until I can determine why Nichole was murdered, I have a single responsibility: delivering Sarah to her family. There is no need to take hurried action. Since the Vicodin's keeping the pain at bay, I expect I have enough time to accomplish my mission. Meanwhile, we're out of danger.

Googling Nichole Atkinson, I soon locate her on the website of the Class of 2008 College Reunion for Reed College. I peruse the predictable reunion photos of thirty-something people chatting with cocktails in their hands. My eye is caught by a picture of a laughing Nichole, younger and healthier than when I'd seen her last. The caption reads "Nichole (Osipovich) Atkinson."

Another reference leads me to the Portland Art Museum staff page. Among the staff photographs is

Nichole—the picture on her ID—captioned with the title of Conservator. I click on *Bio* and read: Nichole Atkinson. B. 1987, Portland, OR. BFA Reed College, Portland. MA Conservation of Works of Art, Institute of Fine Arts, NYU. The Sherman Fairchild Foundation Conservation Fellowship in Objects Conservation, Metropolitan Museum of Art, NY. Since 2013, Portland Art Museum Conservator.

Art conservation. I look it up and find the description fascinating. Preserving artwork for the ages isn't easy, requires years of study. The next citation is for an article in the *Oregonian*, "PAM Art Conservator Brings Silver To Light." I skim. Nichole has restored and brought the Museum's considerable collection of silver decorative arts out of storage and into a specially designed gallery. She had written an accompanying catalogue.

Then I hit pay dirt: from the *Oregonian*, an article dated August 2016. The subject is Lt. Colonel Seth Atkinson, M.D., attached to an Army Reserve unit in Iraq, taking a leave from his practice as a surgeon in Portland. The accompanying photo is of Atkinson, his wife Nichole, and daughter Sarah on the day he deployed. He's in camouflage uniform, standing by an enormous pack. Nichole is in slim black trousers, a short jacket, and boots. He's tall and blonde and embraces her with his left arm. Sarah's in front of them, her daddy's free hand resting on her shoulder. I am instantly jealous of this family grouping; they are so together, such a unit.

Sarah is wearing a wild combination of a plaid dress, striped tights, and miniature flower-patterned Chucks; she has a tiara on her head. She's so lucky—clearly Nichole has allowed her to choose her own clothes. Father and daughter are smiling but Nichole's face is tense with worry, caught at an awkward moment. The article states he will be deployed with his unit for fifteen months.

Daddy will be in Iraq until October. Since Nichole has yet to be identified by law enforcement, he hasn't been notified about his dead wife and missing daughter. Tracing grandparents and other family is another task. I compile a list of names and dates and unpack my new burner phone. Sarah is engrossed in her movie.

In the bathroom, I call QC in Las Vegas.

"Speak!" QC orders.

"Do you recognize my voice?"

There is silence, then: "You fucking bitch. You emailed me you were dead."

"*Going* to be. Important difference."

"You know what that message did to me?" I hear tears in his voice.

"What?" I ask, surprised.

"Jesus. I don't believe you." We are silent. "Cancer, huh?" he asks.

"Yeah. Bad."

"I'm sorry."

"QC, I'm in trouble."

"Where are you?"

I avoid the question. "I need data."

"Seriously? You can't do it yourself?"

"No. All my sources are gone. Can't use my credit cards." Silence on the line, but I hear his mental processors humming: if Olive can't get data, something is seriously wrong.

"I owe you," QC says. "Give it to me."

I reel off the scant information I have on Beau Cassidy, Nichole and Seth Atkinson, and on Sarah. "I need grandparents, relatives; bios, addresses, phone numbers. How do I contact Sarah's daddy in the Army?"

"Email him, idiot."

"Get me an address," I retort. "I'd also like to locate Nichole Atkinson's Toyota. If she has OnStar, or something, can you find it for me?"

"Yes."

"License plate?"

"Yes."

I dictate my new email address and he is gone. I'm stung by his abruptness, but I suppose I don't have any right to hurt feelings. If I had visited QC and explained my death sentence in person, would that have made a difference to him? It had not occurred to me.

Frozen is finished and I don't have to listen to the saccharine music any more. Sarah has hummed with the soundtrack.

It's interesting that she can make noises—humming, screaming, crying, laughing, a sort of gargling purring—but doesn't speak. She was able to spell her name with alphabet soup but when I give her pencil and paper, she merely doodles illegible dots. I memorize the ASL signs for *hello* and *how are you?* and try them out on her but she stares blankly, uncomprehending. The lack of knowledge of sign language might mean she hasn't been mute since birth. She'll have to communicate with actions until she decides to speak.

After returning the DVD to the office, I buckle Sarah into the car seat. On the way to the beach, we stop at Dollar Tree and buy sunscreen and sunglasses, as well as a trowel, bucket, and plastic molds. At Heceta Beach we race across the sand. We're barefoot, wearing shorts and tees. It's rare Oregon coast weather: the sky is blue, the sun is warm. Kids and adults are flying kites and playing with dogs. A group of four women relax in lawn chairs while keeping an eye on their kids jumping and screaming in the freezing surf. The normality of the scene makes me doubt my course of action. Those moms would call the cops, right?

"Want to build a sand castle?" Sarah nods, her eyes obscured by huge blue sunglasses.

"Sunscreen first, please." I slather her arms and legs with SPF 50 and gently smooth it on her face. Sarah points at the sunscreen, then at me. I have to laugh. My cancer-riddled body hardly needs protection but I apply it to please her.

"Thanks. I'm glad you reminded me."

We build a broad round platform, patting the damp sand into place. She uses the cone-like molds to add a ring of towers around the circumference of the platform.

"Shall I make some towers?" No, she doesn't want assistance, is clearly following a blueprint in her head.

I lean forward, elbows on my thighs, staring out to sea. I trust QC will send the info I need. We'd met in college at UNLV and become, well—colleagues. I don't know if we were friends, exactly. As a professional gambler, he earned enough money to pay his tuition while I continued my quest to perfect my techniques for ripping people off; Vegas offers up the most remarkable opportunities. I guess I'd describe us as partners in crime.

After graduation, I'd moved back to my beloved ocean. He'd stayed, hadn't set foot out of Nevada since. QC makes his living searching out information for his clients, but he'd gotten himself into major gambling debt trouble last year and needed a hundred thou. I'd given him the money, no questions asked. After, he told me I'd saved his life and paid me off over the next six months. I hope he stays out of trouble. I won't be around to help him again.

I consider Sarah's father, Dr. Seth Atkinson. When Nichole's calls, texts, and emails to him ceased, hadn't he contacted the authorities? If he had, it would probably have been the Portland police. Would law enforcement connect this query with the unidentified woman who had died on the coast? I envision scenarios wherein Atkinson wouldn't be alarmed at not hearing from his wife for a couple of days. Perhaps he's on a mission where he can't receive personal email. Could be they're having trouble in the marriage, so sporadic contact with Nichole is the norm. But wouldn't she text or email news about Sarah in any case?

I don't know. I have no experience of relationships between men and women except my parents' rotten, drug-addled marriage. I'd emerged from a horrific childhood into adolescence *sans* sex drive or desire for romance, and this had never changed.

I need to curb my impatience; Nichole died only the day before yesterday. It just seems much longer. I have to wait for QC to reply with the data I need to find Sarah's family.

Sarah's castle is finished. She's built tiers and towers and blocks into a complex building. I give her a cellophane packet of American flag toothpicks. Sarah, pleased, sticks a flag atop each tower. I provide her with juice and we contemplate her handiwork. I tell her it is beautiful, that she is a clever designer and a terrific builder. She beams as she sucks on her juicy box straw.

"I'm getting hungry. Do you like fish tacos?" Emphatic nod. I get to my feet, saying, "Let's eat!"

She takes my hand and I pull her up. The first lapping waves of the tide nibble away at the ramparts of her castle. Sarah sighs, as though she knows all good things must come to an end.

I sing along with Pharrell's "Happy" as we drive back into town. Sarah is bopping and clapping, safely secured in her child seat. We've had sun and we've eaten and we feel good. I grin at her in the mirror and she smiles back, wearing her goofy shades. As we near the motel, I'm slowing in the suicide lane to make the left turn when I notice a huge battered Dodge pickup, a king-cab dually, parked askew athwart several slots in front of the office. It's been camo-sprayed in a matte beige and army green, deep-woods fern pattern on a black background.

Something's hinky.

I speed up, change lanes, pull into the McDonald's on the other side of the street, and park in a row of cars. I shut off the engine and watch the motel. The office door crashes against the wall and somebody storms out; I can't see who, as the truck's blocking my sight. I can hear faint yelling. The female clerk emerges and steams down the breezeway, brandishing a cell phone. The other person materializes from behind the truck and advances menacingly, shouting.

Beau Cassidy. It's a beautiful afternoon in a beach town and I'm as terrified as if it's midnight under a Portland bridge. I grip the wheel. How the hell did he get so close, so fast? In alarm I throw the car into gear. Force myself to pause.

Mom, her arms folded, is standing foursquare, holding her ground. Pop joins them. Mom shakes her head, punches in a number on her cell. Cassidy whirls, climbs in the truck, peels out, and screams north. The truck's engine throbs with a deep thunder. I can hear it for a long way as it zooms up the highway. I glance back at Sarah. She is engrossed in a book, paying no attention.

Pop is arguing with Mom and grabbing for the phone, but she twists from his grasp. She advances on him, hopping mad, yelling, gesticulating. Pop retreats into the office. Mom follows.

What the hell just happened? I presume that Pop did indeed see me with a different hair color when we exited our motel room this morning. Shit. Had Cassidy canvassed the strip enquiring about a young blonde woman and a little girl with dark hair? It seemed as though Mom was refusing to give Cassidy information or let him into our room. Has more guts than Pop.

A siren nears. A Lane County Sheriff SUV, lights flashing, speeds up to the motel and brakes to a halt. A female deputy, a tall brunette, emerges. Is it time for me to give Sarah over to the care of the authorities? I'm about to pull out of my parking place when the ugly truck rumbles back down 101, wheels into the motel lot, and stops next to the cruiser. Cassidy emerges and meets the officer. They stand talking, heads together, an intimate pose. They are the same height. Could this deputy be Cassidy's accomplice?

Dashing tears from my eyes, I use my burner phone to take several pictures of the vehicles and the couple across the street. Carefully, I steer the Honda out into the traffic and drive south. I regret the loss of Sarah's toys and now we'll never know if Nancy Drew discovers Mirror Bay's secret. But there's nothing we need at the motel, no reason to return.

Chapter Four

I've been unbelievably stupid. I should have realized Cassidy would assume we'd run to Florence, the first town driving south. I estimate fifteen or so motels in Florence, not so many that a couple of hours of inquiry wouldn't pay off. He'd figure I'd avoid the chain hotels requiring credit cards and he'd concentrate on the mom 'n' pops. The sign on our motel actually says Cash Welcome.

I'm not as exhausted today and oddly enough, feel lighter mentally. Sleep had been healing and the drugs are damping the pain to the level of irritation rather than torture. The scenario in the motel parking lot between Cassidy and the deputy has decided me: I'll continue to protect Sarah until I connect with her family. No more agonizing. Whether I'm right or not about Cassidy's connections, I won't chance it. I'm providing adequate care for Sarah and keeping her out of danger. But I'm not sure about the capabilities or motives of anybody else.

While the model and color of the Honda I'm driving is known, Cassidy is searching for the incorrect plate number. Has he informed the authorities about his discovery of the stolen Honda and are they on alert, too? I doubt it—how would he have explained it? He has no authority to seek information about me. But if the female Lane County deputy is his accomplice, he could utilize computer records through her. I need to dump this car.

I consider fleeing south down the coast. We could go to California. With QC's help, Sarah and I could set up as mother and daughter. We could live in a little apartment by the sea, maybe in Arcata, and be happy together . . .

Sure, Olive—build sandcastles and eat fish tacos till the day you keel over. My happy fantasy fades. I'm going to die. What would happen to Sarah then?

Cassidy would possibly figure that running south is the most logical move. On the other hand, what is logical? He has no clue why I have the child. He'll be puzzled. I'd almost forgotten two people had been involved in abandoning the bodies in the cave. Perhaps Beau's cohort is stationed on the southern edge of Florence, alert to silver Hondas passing by on the highway. There's only one way to cross the river: the Siuslaw River Bridge. Therefore, I decide not to travel south.

What about doubling back, heading north up the coast? Same problem. I have no idea what his accomplice—perhaps the dark-haired sheriff's deputy?—is doing. Driving east to Eugene just feels wrong.

Why this reluctance to go south, or inland to central Oregon? I search my feelings about it and am sure staying on the coast is the right decision. I'm knowledgeable about the environs and I'm more comfortable. The reason for Nichole's murder must lie in Douglas. We'll stay near until I find the answers to my questions. Our most urgent need is to settle somewhere quiet and safe where I can receive QC's information and Sarah can play and heal.

I pull into the St. Vinnie's thrift store lot and park in the middle of a row of cars. I turn to Sarah: would she mind wearing boys' clothes a bit longer? She shrugs, appears to have no interest in fashion or perhaps is more comfortable in boys' clothes. We raid the women's and boys' departments for clothing, sneakers, and daypacks, grab a stack of books, and pay at the counter. In the Honda, we shove everything into the packs and we're out of there.

We weave our way along the streets into Old Town and the docks on the river. Florence is surrounded by sand dunes stretching thirty miles south to Coos Bay, and the Siuslaw River winds west to the sea; thus the docks are inland a couple of miles. Bay Street, location of the original riverside settlement, is the center of the tourist trade where restaurants and bars, souvenir shops, candy stores, and galleries vie for tourist dollars. It's high season and the sidewalks are swarming.

I park the Honda in the lot of an apartment building two blocks from Bay Street. Sarah is engrossed in the pages of *Madeline*. After releasing the trunk, I examine the Beretta lock box. Constructed of steel, it measures about 12" x 8" x 2". I examine the keys on the Honda ring, select the smallest, and fit it into the lock. Turning the key, I lift the lid and laugh out loud. The box houses a dinky pink pistol, about six inches long. Really, Ilsa Christiansen? A pink gun? It looks like a toy but I recognize it's all business, a Beretta Nano 9mm nestled into its foam with a magazine of ammunition. I secure the box in my pack with the keys. We're all set. We abandon the Honda and walk down the hill.

An hour later, sucking on popsicles, we wander along the busy sidewalk. Sarah is inspecting store windows while I scan the traffic for Cassidy's truck and for sheriff's vehicles. I'm wearing my Dead Guy cap and Sarah has a cap with an embroidered red crab captioned I'm Crabby. We wear them with the bills tipped low, and sunglasses. We've purchased a chunk of fudge, bottled water, caramel corn, and T-shirts. Sarah's is tie-dyed pink and purple, script letters spelling out Oregon Coast. My tee is Mountain Dew yellow, blazoned OREGON MAKES ME WET. On our backs are the daypacks carrying our possessions.

I'm laden with a selection of shopping bags and our bodies are arrayed with bright tourist logos. We blend right in with the crowds of flip-flopped families cruising the bay front. We have a lunch of hamburgers, french fries, and juice at a dockside cafe. I toy with the idea of stealing another car. But I believe this is what Cassidy would expect; he'll utilize his sheriff department contact to receive reports of stolen vehicles. I stare out at the broad blue-gray avenue of the Suislaw.

"Let's check out the marina, shall we?" Sarah shoots to her feet. Apparently she's into boats.

As we lean on the railing of the promenade, taking in the activity of the marina, I notice all the children on the docks are wearing flotation vests. Ha! Another car seat-type issue, I surmise. You learn fast, Olive. The kid at the bait shack rents me two life vests. I strap Sarah into hers and add mine to the collection of bags in my hand. I pick up a free tide table and consult it. The tide is about to turn and the Suislaw will be flowing out to sea. Alrighty then. Downriver it is.

I thank him and as we leave, I glance up Bay Street. Cassidy's brutal black camouflage truck cruises past, maybe fifty feet away. His head is turned toward the other side of the street. My heart thumps in concert with the deep engine rumble. We saunter down the runway to the docks, mingling with the other tourists. I'm hoping Cassidy's eye will pass us by, disguised as we are.

Out of sight below, we amble by the moored vessels. Sarah points toward a lovely antique wooden sailboat, forest green and gold; I tell her I admire her taste. Toward the end we come on a fishing boat, the deck crowded with tarps covering unidentifiable lumps. The name of the craft has been whited out and the cabin is crammed with toolboxes and equipment. Nobody seems to be on board. Snugged in at the stern is a tender, a ten-footer cluttered with paint cans, solvent, and brushes. Painted the airy blue of a Stellar's jay, the tiny boat has two benches and a paddle. Someone has presumably been using it to row around to paint the larger craft. It bobs invitingly in the current. In spite of being grubby, the tender is pretty chipper, riding high. It has a stenciled number and a current Oregon sticker on the bow, all nice and legal.

I casually eyeball the other vessels in the vicinity. No bodies sunning themselves, nobody fishing. No strolling families in the immediate vicinity.

I say, "Here we go, buddy," and lift Sarah in. "Sit on the bench, would you please?"

I chuck the pack and shopping bags in the bow and clamber aboard. When I'm balanced, I slide the painting supplies onto the deck of the fishing boat. I retain a rusty gallon can in case we have to bail. Untying the line from the cleat, I push us gently from the dock. Wielding the paddle, I guide the craft into the middle of the boat basin and we float into the open channel of the Siuslaw.

Nobody shouts, "Stop thief!" It's a lovely summer day in Oregon, sunny and pleasant, no breeze here inland. The wind freshens out toward the ocean, but we must not travel as far as the big water. We'd be in real trouble in this dainty toy.

The Siuslaw borders Florence on the west and south, eventually angling out to the Pacific between the pair of jetties. The land on the east side is all municipal, businesses and residential areas fronting the water. The other side marks the boundary of the Oregon Dunes National Recreation Area, government land. The Siuslaw cuts a wide, deep path through the sand, reminding me of the surreal scene in *Lawrence of Arabia* when T. E Lawrence sees an enormous ship sailing across the desert—he'd made it to the Suez Canal.

I steer us closer to the eastern bank. Our craft gently rocks. An osprey flies overhead, its shadow flickering across us. I glance at Sarah. She grins at me, her hand trailing in the water. I return her smile. "Pretty day." She nods vigorously.

We are now being carried along behind the businesses on Bay Street. Cassidy could be viewing the river from any of a dozen shops or restaurants with windows. But I doubt it. He won't figure on my taking a boat but rather that I'll steal another vehicle or catch the bus. If he's hunting for us on the bay front, perhaps we could have fled south in the Honda. It doesn't matter. The die is cast, we're on our way.

The channel curves and we glide into the shadows under the historic Siuslaw River Draw Bridge with its graceful loops and fanciful towers. I point. "Looks like your castle." Sarah agrees.

We lean our heads back and gaze at the understructure, listening to the rumble of traffic. We come out into the sun and I examine the shore. We'll travel as far as possible from Old Town but we must be ashore before reaching the Coast Guard station out toward the rock jetties. Idiot tourists in a teensy tender nearing the big waves of the bar

70

would certainly alarm the authorities. They'd intervene to ensure we wouldn't wash out to sea or crash on the jetties. Danger aside, we'd be discovered, urgently to be avoided.

I study the sun. It's almost dinnertime and I want to be offshore the neighborhood I've chosen at dusk. We're going too quickly. Angling toward the shore where ancient pilings stick up out of the river, I guide the boat into the little forest and tie the line to a piling.

"Are you thirsty?" I uncap a water bottle for her.

She squirms. "You have to pee?" Yes, she does.

Right here, the Sarah-as-boy impersonation is going all wrong. Fortunately no one is in sight at the top of the bank, no vessels floating by, so I help Sarah pull down her shorts and squat over the can. Most of the pee hits the target and I dump it into the river.

Browsing the books purchased at St. Vinnie's, I ask, "Have you read *The Secret Garden*?" Sarah nods with enthusiasm.

"Shall we read it again?" She settles beside me on my bench, lays her head on my lap. Before opening the pages, I take in our surroundings. In spite of being hunted, this is a terrific day. We're sitting in a cute blue boat on a sunny river, securely tied up, with clean wavelets lapping the stern. On the opposite shore, the sculpted, creamy sand drifts are broken by stands of deep green scrub and tall Douglas fir—no buildings, no vehicles, no trash. The bank looms thirty feet above us, verdant with grasses and wildflowers. A flotilla of ducks paddles by. Cormorants dive, swallowing fish down their long gullets. Further out on the river a powerboat burbles by and the wake rocks us gently. An occasional vehicle passes by on the road up above. Sarah is waiting patiently for me to begin and at this moment, I can almost believe I'm happy.

I read to her about the disagreeable English girl being raised in India by amahs. We become enthralled by her tale as she loses her parents and is shipped to England to an uncle whom she's never met. Bit of a parallel to Sarah, the loss of a mother. I wonder if Sarah recognizes this, or if she has any memory of what actually happened to her mom. If she remembers the story, she'll know a happier life awaits Mary Lennox. I look down at Sarah. She is fast asleep.

I'd learned how to paddle a tender at the age of eight, living on a boat with my parents Charlie and Sean in Yaquina Bay. This might seem sort of romantic but the reality was the *Charlie B*, a filthy, ramshackle fishing craft with a minute cabin and two narrow bunks. I had vague memories of an apartment we'd lived in before I began school, but after awhile the boat was our only home. My dad had fished and my mom worked as a barista, but after awhile all they accomplished was drinking. Soon they started on drugs. Now I recognize they had become hopeless tweakers, but at the time I only knew food was scarce, the *Charlie B* never left the dock, and the head was plugged up and overrunning. My mom stopped paying any attention to me and my daddy hadn't noticed me for months. I couldn't talk to them or ask for anything; irritable, restless, and relentlessly cranky, they grew increasingly unhealthy, skinny, itching their skin infections and sores. Their teeth were in horrible shape.

My own appearance grew increasingly scuzzy. I kept my head down at school and minded my own business. In appearance, I didn't look too different from other kids who were homeless and weren't cared for properly, who wore ragged clothes and worn-out shoes. The more prosperous students kept their distance. I had no friends in either group. I heard kids talk about grandparents, aunties, uncles, and cousins. I asked my mom why we had no family. She'd teared up, saying, puzzled, "Don't know where they all went to."

The welfare check arrived once a month. With my mom, I'd climb up the hill to the bank to cash it. I made sure she gave me money immediately to buy groceries. I had to make this sum last as long as I could. I did my best to convince my folks to eat. When the money ran out, I could paddle the tender out into the bay, haul up some crabs for dinner, and cook them up on the galley stove, but only if there were funds to refill the gas cylinder. I became adept at stealing. I shopped at the small grocery store with no surveillance cameras and innocently dodged the attention of the manager. I always bought an inexpensive item, with groceries secreted in my shabby daypack.

In decent weather, I curled up in a corner of the deck where I could do my homework. In poor weather, doing schoolwork was impossible, as extra visitors were often crowded into the cabin, partying and raucous. There was loud music and the gross smell of cigarettes and weed, and the reek of too many humans in a cramped, unventilated space. I learned to tell the difference between the dopers and the meth heads, perfected picking pockets in the tight, awful cabin of the *Charlie B*. I stole whatever I could winkle out of the pockets of stoners, targeted the tweakers when they inevitably crashed. On party nights, I couldn't sleep inside. I had nowhere to call my own except the deck.

I spent my hours after school in the public library, studying, reading, napping, and staying warm. Since Mom had lost the key to the women's bathroom and showers in the parking lot of the marina, I kept clean as best I could in the ladies' room at the library. I hadn't much time as somebody was always knocking on the door, rattling the doorknob. If another woman entered the marina facilities, I could slip in and grab a shower. But sometimes I had to wait forever to use the toilet, especially at night. Boat people don't take kindly to folks pooping into the harbor. And I didn't dare request to borrow the head on neighboring craft; on their best day, my folks could not be called good neighbors.

One afternoon, I had to poop so badly I slipped in behind the shrubs bordering the shore drive. I'd dropped my jeans when a siren whooped and an amplified, outraged voice yelled, "Hey, girl, you can't shit in public. Get the hell out of there." I squeezed out a final turd, zipped up my pants, and ran, terrified and humiliated, glancing panicked at the sheriff's cruiser.

I became ultra-careful, using the school bathrooms and the library. I memorized the locations of restrooms at public buildings: the marine science center, resort hotels, city hall, restaurants. I walked everywhere, in all kinds of crappy weather.

I had one friend. She was a librarian. Her nametag said—I swear it—Anna Goodreade, Assistant Director. Miss Goodreade recommended books she thought I'd like and often she shared her lunch or a snack with me. She was, she told me, thirty-eight, unmarried, from Seattle. She had no desire to live anywhere but Newport, adored her snug cottage up the hill with a view of the boat basin. She had brown shiny hair, a pleasant freckled face without makeup, and wore jeans and boots with a tee and blazer. She always had on earrings, and a scarf around her neck. She smelled fresh, like Ivory soap. Miss Goodreade smiled whenever she saw me, which made me feel like somebody important. She let me nap in the scratchy armchair in a little-visited corner of the library, waking me up at closing time and escorting me out the front door.

One night, as my folks were hosting a bunch of druggies in the cabin, I curled up in my Disney *Nightmare Before Christmas* sleeping bag on the cold deck of the boat.

Soon, I couldn't hold it anymore. I scuttled up the ramp to the ladies' room. Locked, of course, the parking lot deserted. I hopped from foot to foot, in agony. If I used the bushes, would that cop humiliate me again?

A friend of my dad's, Tom, rounded the corner, startled to see me. "Hello there, little one, what you doin' up here?" Tom was about my dad's age, tall, skinny, with dirty blond hair in a ponytail. He worked on the *Blue Pacific*, a ninety-foot trawler moored on the end of the dock. He was one of the guys partying with my parents on the *Charlie B*.

I danced in place. "I gotta go. Mom lost the bathroom key."

Tom said, "Well, hey, Olive, I got my key, you can use the men's head. I'll keep watch and won't let anyone in."

I followed him around the building, where he unlocked and held the men's room door for me. "In you go." I dashed for the stall, bare feet freezing on the wet concrete floor. I heard the door clang shut.

I did my business and came out of the stall. But Tom wasn't outside, watching. Tom was leaning against the door, arms folded, waiting for me.

Sarah stirs in my lap and sits up, yawning. The sun is sinking toward the dunes and it's time to float on. I untie the rope and nudge the tender out into the current. We glide past the next subdivision. Suitable, but too close to the main part of town. I'm hunting for an enclave further out toward the jetties. We pass scrub woods and draw even with a line of larger residences. The bank is steep here and we can no longer see what's up top.

Oyster-gray clouds have moved in from the ocean, obscuring the sunset. It is dusk and the air has grown chill. I run aground on a narrow sandy beach. Stepping out into the shallows, I wait, listening. Faint sounds filter down from far above: a lawnmower, kids yelling with exuberance, a dog barking. Neighborhood sounds. I haul the tender up on the sand.

Sarah shivers. I boost her out onto the scanty margin of sand, remove her flotation device, and toss it into the boat with mine. I dig into her daypack for her jacket, hold it for her to put on, and zip it up. I offload our packages and load everything into the daypacks. I strew the colorful shopping bags into the bottom of the boat.

I gaze fondly at our sturdy craft. "Say bye-bye, Sarah," I whisper. "It's a sweet boat." She pats the bow.

I fling the paddle into the river, bail several cans of water into the tender, and shove it out into the river where it is gradually caught in the current. Sarah waves goodbye. Hopefully, it will float out to sea, but most likely will crash on the jetty.

Always obfuscate.

From the bottom of the riverbank, it's a tough climb to the top. I boost Sarah across a piled barrier of boulders and cast about for a way through the thick bushes growing wild along the Siuslaw. Finding a faint trail, I grip Sarah's hand and pull her up, testing my footing with each step. I slip on slick mud and drop Sarah's hand as I seize the branches of a thorny blackberry. Sarah makes a distressed squeak as she slides slowly away from me. I reach out and clasp her arm, hauling her up to my side. She cries out but scrambles up level with me, plants her sandals in the muck, and holds on. I stroke her arm, breathlessly apologizing for hurting her. She pats my cheek. Tough kid.

We rest a bit, breathing heavily. We resume climbing and finally my eyes rise above the bank. I peer at a dark sweeping lawn leading up to a well-lit, contemporary McMansion. This side is all windows. Uneasily, I remember the barking dog. A woman inside passes the windows. I follow her progress through the house like an audience watching a play. She ends up in the kitchen, where she slices something green at a counter.

Sarah and I slither over the crest to the grass and lay heaving. I gasp, "You're a great climber, Sarah."

We have to find an unoccupied dwelling, preferably one for sale. I'm worried though—this is a rich neighborhood, which means security systems.

"We're gonna crawl to the next house. Pretend you're Dora exploring, yeah?" She giggles and we set off. And at that moment the woman opens the French doors and a huge bounding shape gallops across the yard toward us.

I jerk Sarah to her feet. "Run!" I glance behind us. It's a Great Dane the size of a Shetland pony and he's gaining on us.

The woman yells, "Atlas! Stay by the house!" I'm sure she can't see us flitting across her big-ass lawn.

Predictably, Atlas ignores her. He's almost on us as I ram into a wooden fence. I hoist Sarah and we levitate over the barrier. I land hard and painfully; Sarah is cushioned by my body. Atlas sits wheezing on the other side of the fence. I can almost hear him going, "Un-hrunh?" in his tiny Scooby brain.

We struggle to our feet and sprint, clambering over a pile of river rock into yet another yard. And another. Four houses later, we pause, panting. I clutch my stomach in sudden agony and topple to the ground. The dog hasn't followed us. I attempt to separate my hand from Sarah's but she's clamped on tight. She's shaking. I dig into my pocket for the Vicodin, pop the lid one-handed, and swallow a pill.

In the ambient light, I see Sarah's face is scrunched up with fear, but she's not crying. Or screaming. I give her the Tic Tacs. "Appropriate for kids," I grunt.

She lets go of my hand, shakes a candy out, and hands me the box. Subsiding, I wait for the drug to kick in. Sarah gazes questioningly into my face.

"It's fine, honey. Just a tummy ache."

Sarah snuggles up and I hug her, whispering, "You're not only fast, you're really brave. Atlas was a humungous dog, but you know? He wasn't dangerous, just curious. I don't think he's very bright." I make the Scooby noise. She relaxes. She's doing unbelievably well. Still, maybe in the future she'll be telling her shrink about her bad scare with the big dog.

I survey the house, an unlighted, angular silhouette against the sky. After a few moments, I'm able to get to my feet. We approach it quietly, hand-in-hand, through the longish grass. Good clue—means the lawn isn't mowed often, in all likelihood signaling absentee owners. We circle past extensive plantings to the front of the house. I stand in the shadows and observe a dimly lit cul-de-sac of four newish, two-story homes situated on expansive lots with professionally-tended landscaping. Peaceful, no cars parked on the street.

Aha—a Coldwell-Banker sale sign mounted on the lawn. I don't spot any security company decals. Doesn't mean much. Why would you put those on your house, anyway? All they do is inform us thieves what brand system you have installed. All of a sudden a light blinks on in the window nearest us. We hit the ground. No sound. Nothing moves. I peep into a gap in the blinds—an empty laundry room. Illumination is from a ceiling fixture, probably on a timer.

I whisper, "We'll stay here for the night. But we need be ready to dash if we have to." Her eyes widen. She's awfully young to be receiving an extensive education in breaking and entering. It'll be somebody else's job to discuss the ethical ramifications with her.

I grab a rock from a nearby flowerbed, wrap it in my jacket, aim, and punch the window glass. Shards fall to the floor. I reach my arm in, unfasten the latch, and raise the window.

We rapidly retreat to the end of the yard and crouch in the shadows for thirty minutes, but neither the cops nor a security company shows up. We circle the house. The street is empty.

I throw my jacket onto the windowsill, heave Sarah up and in, and slide in myself. We pause, but the house is silent. It seems to be uninhabited, no clicks or whirring or hums. Sneaking out of the laundry room, we follow a hall into a cathedral-ceilinged living area encompassing living room, dining room, and kitchen. I can see by ambient light that the soaring space is nicely furnished, but unlike the scruffy beach cottage we'd found further north, it's curiously impersonal. A two-story wall of long windows faces the channel below and the dunes and the sea. It is an unbelievably beautiful view, sparse lights twinkling and the surface of the river glinting. We trudge up a wide staircase, snooping five bedrooms with baths, expensively furnished but with no personal things strewn about. I realize it must be a vacation rental.

When I'm satisfied the house is tenantless, we return to the kitchen. The fridge is empty. In a counter drawer I locate the steel cylinder of a flashlight and switch it on. Sarah tugs at my hand, peers up at me, wriggles her bottom. I lead her into the powder room near the kitchen. Sarah pees and flushes.

I'm flying high. I love this, creeping other people's homes. But Sarah is drooping, exhausted and hungry. She doesn't think it's fun. I come back to earth, fasten her jeans. In the kitchen, I pour her a tumbler of water and explore the cupboards. She drinks thirstily.

A table lamp in the living room suddenly lights up, startling us both. In the kitchen, the window facing toward the cul-de-sac has a shade. No one can spy us unless they are in the backyard. The two-story window wall can't be covered. I switch on the hood light illuminating a Viking six-burner. There's not much in the kitchen to eat. The cupboard nearest the stove contains salt, pepper, spices, cooking oil. In the next, a weird variety of canned goods: tomato sauce, chicken soup, black beans, fruit cocktail, a lone can of root beer. A half-bag of rice. Provisions renters most likely left after their vacations.

"How about black beans and rice?" Sarah shrugs between sips.

"Want to try it?"

Sarah shakes her head no and wanders into the living room. Standing by a cushy sofa, she unfolds the throw draped on the arm. She tucks one end under a cushion and extends the other to the coffee table, where she anchors it with a stone pelican. She pushes two sofa cushions and another throw before her and disappears into her tent. I hover nearby, wondering what to do, but soon realize that clearly she's on her very last nerve. She's constructed a den in which to retreat.

I open a can of soup, pour a mug, nuke it. Put fruit cocktail into another, with a spoon. I approach Sarah's hideout and leave the food outside the entrance.

"Soup, Sarah. Nice warm soup."

A small grubby hand appears and the soup is dragged into the depths. In a moment, the other mug disappears, too.

Okay, then. I'll give her some alone time.

In the kitchen, I cook rice. Heat the beans and pile it on rice. Leave a bowl of rice for Sarah by her shelter. Sitting in the living area, I stare out into the night, struggling to concentrate as I pick at my plate. I'm exhausted and aching. Badly need to rest and regroup.

In the kitchen I fill a glass with water and drink it with another Vicodin. Pop the tab of the root beer and set it by Sarah's tent with a square of Old Town fudge. Use the powder room, leaving the light on for Sarah. Duck into the laundry room to switch on the hot water heater. I unplug the lamps on timers and stretch out on the sofa nearest Sarah's. We're secure for now. The Vicodin takes me down.

Chapter Five

In the morning, I move cautiously from room to room, peering out windows, checking the perimeter in vain—the house is completely blanketed in a dense cottony fog. Venturing slowly out across the lawn, I listen intently. The immediate neighborhood is hushed, no cars, no one walking about in the cul-de-sac. It's mid-week. Probably renters and absentee owners from Eugene or Portland visit only on the weekends. I seek out the garage but unfortunately it's empty of vehicles. Uneasy, I stand in the living room listening. The house feels insulated. Wrapped in the thick layer of fog, we are invisible. Dangerous thinking, Olive, you can be discovered any time.

In the hall leading off the kitchen, I spy a padlocked door opposite the laundry room. Most likely this is the room in which the owners store the things they use when visiting the house: food, booze, the nice sheets and towels, all the luxuries they keep safe from renters. This immediately sets my antennae tingling.

In the kitchen, I find a pair of scissors in the utensil drawer. I retrieve the empty root beer can from Sarah's lair. Puncturing the side of the can, I cut around to make a flat piece of aluminum, scissor out a square about two inches by two inches, and further cut it into a blocky letter M. I fold up the outer legs of the M and round off the center support. Now I have a strong rectangle of metal from which protrudes a tongue.

In the hallway, I bend the protrusion around the shackle and slide it down inside the lock. After jiggering it for a few seconds, the lock springs open. Inside the substantial storage room I discover a treasure trove: a refrigerator, a freezer, and shelves stuffed with goodies. I load milk, cream cheese, and frozen bagels from Zabar's into a nearby basket. From the shelves I grab a bag of Jamaican Blue Mountain, two boxes of cereal, and add in a bottle of cranberry juice. From a cache of art supplies I load up a sketchbook, markers, and crayons. I dump it all in the kitchen and brew up a carafe of superior coffee.

Taking my mug of coffee upstairs to the master bedroom, I turn on the TV. The Portland morning news is on. After the weather, the story I've been dreading begins: Sarah's mother has been identified. The photograph from her Portland Art Museum ID card is posted beside the newscaster, who reports that when Nichole Atkinson failed to show up to work after her mini-vacation to the coast, people at the Museum had been worried. Nichole had scheduled an important meeting. Staff members had tried her cell and had gone by the house, to no avail. No

Nichole, no car. A staff person remembered the item on the previous night's broadcast about the unidentified woman brought to shore from the surf, and called the sheriff's department. After the sheriff's office received Nichole's PAM ID photo, the dreaded identification had been made. Authorities had contacted the military to notify her husband abroad.

The blond newscaster stares worriedly into the camera: "Concern now is for Nichole Atkinson's missing daughter Sarah, last seen in this cafe in Philomath." A shot of Eats and Treats, a corner cafe on the main drag of the village, appears. "Sarah is five years old and will be in kindergarten in the fall." The picture switches to a snapshot of Sarah on a swing, long braids flying. "The Sheriff's Department requests the public to call the number at the bottom of the screen if anyone has information on the missing girl."

Now my driver's license photo comes up. As do all people in DMV pics, I look disgruntled and edgy. "Police are also seeking school district employee Olive Wiley whose car was found abandoned at the beach access parking lot where the body of Nichole Atkinson was discovered. Wiley also has not reported for work and has not been seen since Thursday." The newscast finishes and I turn it off.

Pussyfooting down the stairs into the living room, I peek into Sarah's tent. She's fast asleep, breathing quietly— good. She's slept for eight hours and I'm sure she needed it badly. I sink into an upholstered chair and stare out the vast window wall before me. The fog is shifting inland. To the west is the wide river, beyond it the dunes. I can see all the way out to sea. To the northwest, the river bends and flows out between long jetties. The sky is bright ceramic cobalt and the wind is blowing hard. Wavelets corrugate the surface of the river and wild surf beats on the huge rocks of the jetty, spray spuming high into the air. The blue dingy has probably been reduced to splinters by now. To my left glides the rapidly retreating wall of fog.

Sleepy-eyed and tousled, Sarah emerges from her tent and stumbles over to my chair. I gather her in and she allows me to position her on my lap. Hugging her tight, I kiss the top of her head.

"Did you sleep well, little Sarah?" She is silent against my chest. We sit companionably together.

"Do you need to use the bathroom?" Sarah shakes her head no.

"Did you get up in the night all on your own?" Tiny nod.

"Sarah, you could have woken me up." She pats my tummy, looks up into my face.

"Oh, cookie, my tummy's okay. And I got a good night's sleep, too." Sarah is reassured.

"Breakfast?" Sarah leaps to her feet and leads the way to the kitchen.

After juice, cereal, and bagels, we climb the stairs and I draw a warm bath with lots of bubbles in a vast tub next to windows overlooking the river. I strip off her clothes and am dismayed to see a dark bruise on her arm from my grab in the climb up the riverbank.

I kiss her boo-boo, telling Sarah how sorry I am. She splashes in the tub, ducks under the water, and emerges, throwing bubbles everywhere. In the shower, placed conveniently by the tub, I use a lovely variety of toiletries from the unlocked closet.

After Sarah is clean and dressed, she settles at the coffee table with the art supplies and draws using colored markers. I sit at the dining table with the tablet, where I can also see the flat screen TV. I mute it and wait for the news.

On a sideboard is laid the "Welcome To Our Home" three-ring-binder for renters, and I locate the Wi-Fi password for the house. I open my email. QC has come through. Lots of attachments, but his message is short and distant in tone. I infer he hasn't forgiven me.

"Here's the stuff you requested. I do hope it is adequate for your needs." It's signed, merely, Q, with a P.S. "You might have missed the article on your Beau Cassidy, since they spelled his name wrong. But it came up when I searched for Osipovich, Nichole's maiden name."

I visit the URL and read a three-week old article:

News Source 15 - KGNE Eugene

Douglas Firefighter Saves Dog With Mouth-To-Mouth Resuscitation

LINCOLN COUNTY, OREGON - A German Shepherd survived a fire Monday afternoon in Douglas due to a quick-thinking firefighter.

The fire broke out just after 4 p.m. Monday afternoon at a home owned by a recently deceased man, Leonid Osipovich, on Grey Whale Drive in Douglas.

According to the neighbor who had been caring for the dog since Osipovich's death last month in a car accident, the responding firefighters were true heroes.

"I'm so grateful to the firefighters for rescuing Carl," praised Luanne Greene. "I'd left him in his own garage while I drove up to Newport to run errands. When I got back, the driveway was full of fire trucks."

Firefighter and EMT Bo Cassidy was credited with pulling the dog out of the smoke and for performing mouth-to-mouth resuscitation on the dog, saving his life.

"We're glad he got the dog out," stated Douglas Fire Chief Martin Ponsler. "No one else was in the house and no firefighters were injured, so any time you can walk away from one of these with no injuries, it's a successful fire fight."

Carl the German Shepherd was taken to Coast Animal Clinic where reportedly he is in satisfactory condition, thanks to the actions of EMT Cassidy. Luanne Greene stated that from now on she'll keep Carl safe in her own house.

The home has about $90,000 worth of damage to the garage and laundry room, according to Chief Ponsler. He said it was too early to speculate on the cause of the fire.

Just like that, there's the connection: Nichole's father linked to Beau Cassidy through the article about the fire at the Osipovich home. Maybe Beau Cassidy isn't all bad; he'd saved a dog in a pretty intimate manner. The story doesn't quite jibe, though, with a man who'd murder a woman. Unless he was one of those bubbas who value his dog, pickup, and gun over any woman.

I read an article from the *Newport News Times*: Leonid Osipovich had had a heart attack and drove off the river road into the estuary east of Douglas. He had died before rescuers could get him out of the sunken car. It says he is survived by daughter Nichole Atkinson, granddaughter Sarah, and Lt. Colonel Seth Atkinson, son-in-law; and also lists relatives in New York.

The next attachment from QC is his general summary. As I already knew, Nichole's maiden name was Osipovich; she was an only child. Her father Leonid Osipovich, address on Grey Whale Drive in Douglas, had died at the age of 78 in a car accident. Leonid's wife of forty years, Caterina, had died seven years before, survived by a sister, niece, and nephew in Florida. Three siblings of Leonid Osipovich are still living in the New York area; no relatives in Oregon.

Before retirement, Leonid had lived in New York, made his living as a metalsmith and jewelry designer for a jewelry company in Brooklyn, website url given. He and Caterina had moved to Oregon when Leonid had retired. Why did they pick Douglas instead of Portland, where their daughter and her family lived? Perhaps after vacationing along the coast, Leonid and Caterina had fallen in love with its rugged beauty, as so many travelers do when visiting the ocean. QC has provided an address in Portland for Nichole and Seth Atkinson, the website for Atkinson's surgical practice, and his birthplace, birthdate, credit rating, details of education, and two business-related articles on his clinic. Parents both alive and living in southern California; no family in Oregon.

Sarah's maternal grandparents are both dead. Her paternal grandparents are a long distance away; they're not likely to be much help at present, but I can always call them if necessary. There's an email address and phone for Lt. Colonel Atkinson, who hasn't had time to return to the states from Iraq.

I decide to wait and contact Dr. Atkinson later. QC had garnered two more articles from Oregon newspapers on the silver collection curated by Nichole at the Portland Art Museum but they impart nothing more than had been covered in the one I'd already read.

Next is the information on Beau Cassidy: born in 1986, Astoria, Oregon. Current address in Douglas, Oregon. Single. Part-time position, Douglas Fire District; also works at Pro-Build Lumber, Newport. Parents: Nita and Shane Cassidy. Father owner of Astoria Pawn; mother a nurse at Columbia Memorial. One female sibling, living in Seattle. Beau had graduated from Astoria High School in 2003; had an AA degree in Fire Science from Clatsop Community

College; certification as an EMT; had volunteered with the Astoria Fire Department before moving to the Douglas district. Cassidy's phone and email are listed.

I ponder Cassidy's bio. He's well-qualified, yet is employed only part-time with the DFD. Martin and Jill Ponsler, the full-time staffers, are near retirement age. Perhaps Beau is being groomed to take Martin's place as Chief after their retirement? One vehicle registered to Cassidy: a black 2000 Dodge Ram 3500 pickup. The truck I'd spotted him driving.

QC has included the Oregon license plate number of Nichole's 2012 Toyota RAV4. She's enrolled in Safety Connect and he's tracked the Toyota's location. On the map attached, it shows her SUV parked in the Siuslaw National Forest east of Yachats. I bring up the map on my tablet and see it's five miles or so through the labyrinth of forest service and logging roads from Granddad's house. I find Cassidy's house on the map—he lives in town, two blocks from the firehouse.

I google the Lane County Sheriff's Office. Deputy Camas Cates is the sole female deputy listed on the staff roster. No photo. Therefore, I can only assume she is the deputy whom I'd witnessed speaking with Cassidy at the motel. Bio states she was born in 1984 in Camas, Washington, which would make her thirty-two. Earned a degree from Lewis and Clark in Portland; law enforcement academy; went to work for Clark County

Sheriff's Department in her home county. Cates was hired by Lane County Oregon in 2013.

Sarah has been contentedly working at the coffee table and now she appears by my chair, drawings in hand. I study her sketches. The papers are covered with lopsided ovals in bright colors. Odd. I give her a quizzical glance and she hammers the papers with her fist. The first depicts an oval on its side. It is yellow and has festoons of what seem to be brown flowers decorating its surface. An Easter egg? But from one end, three short lines protrude. A bug? But then I remember the plastic egg she'd decorated in the motel. The ovals must be eggs.

Sarah impatiently turns the paper vertically, poking it emphatically. Now the oval sits like a fat rocket ship on a tripod launching pad. I notice she's rendered a thick belt around the middle.

"Humpty Dumpty?" She slaps her hands to the sides of her head in agony.

"I take it I'm wrong." Sarah nods with great vigor. She gives me the second drawing. This oval is colored solid blue. It has curved legs connected together by something linear, similar to an orange rope. It lists to the right on curved uneven legs.

An image flickers in my mind and is gone.

Placing the third drawing directly before me, she slaps her hand on top of it. Moving in front of me, placing her hands on my knees, she puts her face near mine, staring like a little wide-eyed owl.

I smile. "These are important?" She nods.

What the heck are they? In this image, a yellow egg-shape studded with red and green dots lies horizontally with the wider end sliced off, so it has the appearance of a hollow kettle. Scattered about are odd shapes, most are roughly rectangular and others squiggly.

"Did the worms crawl out of the egg?" I ask.

Sarah shakes her head, tears welling up in her eyes.

"I'm sorry, cookie. I don't get it. But you did nice sketches." I glance again at the third drawing. Nope, nothing is making any sense. I return to the first one. Another mini frisson of deja vu.

Sarah slips from my lap and stumps determinedly up the stairs. As I follow after her, she veers into the bathroom where she had her bubble bath. She stands at the counter, pulling out drawers, one after the other. Reaching in, she removes a pair of scissors, nail clippers, and nail file. A comb. A toothbrush. She lines these up on the countertop and glances up at me. I shrug, not understanding.

She gathers up the toiletry tools and starts for the door.

"Wait, cookie, let me carry them, okay?" Relinquishing them, Sarah leads me downstairs.

I put the implements on the table. On the drawing of the yellow egg with its truncated end, Sarah places the tools on top of the rectangular and wormy shapes.

I view the array. "These are what came out of the egg?" She indicates yes, with a little moue of exasperation at my thick-headedness. *Duh.*

Decorated eggs. Hollow eggs. Eggs with things inside of them. The fleeting memory solidifies. Hadn't I recently read about someone who'd discovered a golden egg at a flea market, an egg worth millions?

I google *golden egg.* Entries begin with the story of "The Goose That Laid The Golden Egg." I amend the search to *antique golden egg.* A citation is headed, "Scrap metal dealer finds $33 million Fabergé golden egg." Sarah and I gasp as a color photo of a gorgeous gold egg mounted on an elaborate stand pops into view. Sarah points, grinning.

Huh. Golden eggs. I type in *Fabergé eggs* and hit *Images.* The page comes up, hundreds of Easter eggs fashioned from gold, silver, enamel, gems. Fabulous, unbelievably ornamented eggs, most supported by fancy jeweled legs. Others lay on their sides, opening in the middle to reveal objects within. Sarah stabs decisively at the tablet screen with her forefinger.

"These are what you want me to see?" She nods with emphasis.

I browse the articles on the history of the Fabergé company. It's fascinating reading. I read out loud but Sarah soon loses interest and goes back to her drawing.

The House of Fabergé was founded in 1842 by Gustav Fabergé. The company came into its own after his son Carl became head of the St. Petersburg family jewelry business in 1882 and expanded to Moscow, Kiev, Odessa, and London, serving an elite, wealthy clientele worldwide. The firm served as Imperial Court Jewelers to the Russian Tsars from 1885 until 1917, the year the Tsarist autocracy was shattered by the Russian Revolution. The famous Fabergé Easter Eggs—fabulous frivolities wrought in gold and jewels—had been commissioned by Tsars Alexander III and Nicholas II as Easter presents for family members. Dubbed Imperial Easter Eggs, Fabergé master metalsmiths had designed and fabricated a total of fifty Imperial Eggs for the royal family.

The first Easter egg, *The Hen Egg*, was created for Empress Maria Fedorovna. Compared to later eggs, it was relatively simple: a gold egg enameled eggshell white opening to a gold yolk, which contained a jeweled chicken, opening to a gold and diamond replica of the Imperial Crown. Most likely, Carl Fabergé had been inspired by the humble Matryoshka nesting dolls of Russia. Subsequent Easter eggs all concealed a 'surprise': a ship, a carriage, a model of St. Petersburg, portraits. As the years passed, the eggs grew in size and ostentation.

Each egg took about a year to fabricate in a Fabergé workshop. Sometimes the egg was designed by Fabergé himself, and drawings and measurements prepared. The appropriate gems were sought. The surprise for each egg was commissioned. A workmaster was appointed to supervise a team of metalsmiths, and the egg was fabricated step-by-step, each process performed by an expert in that particular field. In this way, the egg gradually moved from member to member of the team to completion.

Unfortunately, the Fabergé eggs so beloved by the Imperial family became prime symbols of the wasteful spending by the Tsars as the rest of the country suffered. After the Russian Revolution, Fabergé and his family, who had served royalty, were forced to flee the country, his businesses in Russia nationalized.

The Bolsheviks ransacked the palaces for riches. A few of the eggs disappeared as loot, while others were stored in the Kremlin's vaults and seemingly were forgotten until 1927 when Stalin, needing to finance his regime, began cashing in Russian artworks and valuables. Many of the eggs were sold abroad as part of the 'treasures into tractors' scheme to raise money. Originally, the plan was for the eggs to be broken apart for the gems and melted down for the gold but foreign interest in the Imperial Eggs as artworks allowed them to be kept intact. Even though Stalin was credited with saving the eggs from destruction through sheer venality, the eggs had been let go for ridiculously low prices. Fifty Imperial eggs had been fabricated, most now residing in collections and museums all over the world, each valued at million of dollars.

Seven of the Imperial Eggs had been lost over time.

Myriad stories from 2012 describe the discovery of one of these misplaced treasures. An American precious metals scrap dealer came across a gold trinket at a Midwest flea market and purchased it for $14,000. Intending to sell it for the value of the materials, for minimal profit, it was fortunate he did some online research: he discovered he was in possession of the long-mislaid *Third Imperial Easter Egg*, its surprise intact, a bejeweled watch. After partnering with Wartski, the famed London family firm of antique dealers specializing in Russian works of art, especially Fabergé, the scrap dealer realized what is purported to be $33 million from a deal with a private collector brokered by Wartski.

Fucking A!

Scrutinizing the photo of the newly discovered *Third Imperial Easter Egg*, I marvel that anyone could mistake it as anything but an example of the finest craftsmanship, its refinement indicative of an exceptional art object. Perhaps the yellow-gold egg standing on end on its corbelled legs and lion's paw feet had been dulled with filth and grease, hiding the quality of the workmanship. I recall that Nichole's expertise was restoring artifacts such as this. Whoever had been hired to restore the egg had probably found its presence on the workbench astounding; that specialist had perhaps considered bringing the *Third Imperial Easter Egg* back to original condition the professional experience of a lifetime.

In the photograph, the refurbished artwork is splendid, the perfect ridged surface of the egg gleaming, encircled by gold garlands suspended from cabochon sapphires topped with rose diamond-set bows. When the large diamond on the front is pressed, I read, the egg smoothly opens to reveal a ladies' watch—an extremely valuable Vacherin Constantin—which swivels upright, transforming the egg into a table clock. I'm astounded to understand that the diminutive egg is only 3.2 inches tall, about the size of an actual hen's egg; its presence is monumental on the screen.

Researchers uncovered the fact that the *Third Imperial Egg* had somehow traveled from Russia to New York City, where it had been purchased in 1964 for $2,450. Apparently neither the Parke Bernet auction house nor the buyer had recognized the object as an Imperial Egg. *Oops, Parke Bernet!* The egg had vanished from the public eye until it had been purchased at the flea market. Where the hell had it been all those years?

Leonid Osipovich had been a metalsmith, daughter Nichole an expert on the restoration of historic metal artworks. Obviously this family connection through fine metalsmithing must somehow relate to Sarah's drawings of Fabergé eggs. On the website of the Brooklyn firm where Leonid had been employed, I get an eyeful of jewels, enamel and gold. I'll be damned: he'd designed and crafted eggs for a company licensed to create and sell *reproduction* Fabergé eggs. I click on the *Imperial Eggs* menu, then on *Imperial Coronation Egg*. Along with a history of the Faberge original, the site provides photos of a yellow-enameled egg draped with gold-colored swags. In the interior of the egg nestles a reproduction of the Coronation Coach. Price is $2,500. As the site warns, no precious metals or gems were used in making the duplicates.

Continuing my reading, I learn about another of the lost Imperial Eggs named the *Nécessaire Egg*, crafted from gold in 1889 and crusted with emeralds, diamonds, and rubies. I read the definition of a *nécessaire*: a receptacle for toiletry and grooming tools, also called an *étui*.

I perk up—this is intriguing. The Fabergé *Nécessaire Egg* had contained a thirteen-piece kit of diamond-encrusted accessories and toilet items, possibly scissors, mirror, comb, toothpick, tongue scraper, earwax spoon, nail file, tweezers, and so on. It had been recorded in 1952 as being for sale in a London shop – Wartski, in fact. It was sold for £1,250 to an unidentified man who bought it for cash. The *Nécessaire* was never publicly seen again.

On the Wartski website, I read a history of the *Nécessaire Egg* and inspect the sole surviving photo of it (no drawings had been discovered either), a dim, pixilated, black and white image of an egg enfolded in a swath of velvet with only the end visible. The *Nécessaire Egg* was commissioned by Alexander III for Easter 1889, and was invoiced by Fabergé on May 4th as *Nécessaire Egg, 1900 roubles*.

If no clear photos of the *Nécessaire* were in existence, how did Sarah know what it looked like in order to make a likeness of it? Quite a conundrum.

I pore over a black and white photograph of one of the Fabergé workshops, a long hall with one wall lined with windows. I count at least forty men in the room, most seated at curious scalloped wooden worktables comprising seven jeweler's stations. The metalsmiths are crowded around tables covered by a confusion of tools. The several workshops of Fabergé had constructed thousands of pieces of jewelry besides the Imperial Eggs and kept hundreds of jewelers employed. Could one of these men be Leonid Osipovich? No, the timing was off. Osipovich had died at age 78, so he would have been born in 1938, much too late to have been employed as a metalsmith on the original eggs. What about Leonid's father, could he have been one of the metalsmiths at Fabergé? If he had been, say, thirty years old when the *Nécessaire* had been crafted, that would have made him seventy-nine when Leonid had been born. Weirder things had happened. Or perhaps it had been Leonid's grandfather who had some kind of connection to Fabergé?

Bringing up the blurred, indistinct photo of the *Nécessaire*, I ask Sarah to come over and look. She stares at the screen, thumb in mouth. I place Sarah's drawing and the pile of toiletry tools by the computer.

"Is this what you drew?" Sarah is confused. "This is a pretty poor photograph," I apologize, "but could it be the same as what you have drawn?"

Sarah shakes her head, uncertain.

I show her a picture of a non-Fabergé egg, identified as a 17th century French *nécessaire*, with toiletry articles spilling out from its interior. It is historically different in design than the Imperial Easter Eggs, Baroque and a bit clunky.

"Is this one similar?" Sarah nods, then changes her mind, shakes her head no. She wanders off to finish drawing her picture of a brown dog. Must be Carl. The dog Cassidy had saved.

Could the MacGuffin in this murder mystery be a Fabergé Easter egg? Like the sculpture in Huston's film (and Hammett's novel) *The Maltese Falcon*, maybe a valuable object had been the impetus for Nichole's murder. The missing *Nécessaire*? Money seemed a likely motive. Beau certainly doesn't have much in the way of income.

Nah, I thought, don't be ridiculous. Too fantastical to be possible. Why would one of the vanished treasures of the world be stashed in Oregon? Surely there must be a more prosaic reason for Nichole to have been killed.

That evening, soon after Sarah has crawled into her tent, a hand holding *The Secret Garden* appears from underneath the blanket. I lie on the floor and read to her until, peeking under the throw, I see she is asleep. Swallowing another Vicodin, I consider our next move. I haven't yet contacted

Dr. Seth Atkinson. I don't want to talk to him right now or even think about him. I'll mull over this egg situation. I curl up and fall asleep, exhausted.

Chapter Six

Sometime in the deepest night, I awaken to see Sarah silhouetted before the windows. I click on the flashlight and aim it at her knees. Her face, contoured by light from beneath, is contorted, her throat working, her eyes blank, as though she is sleepwalking. She utters a cry of despair. I gather her up and she spiders her arms and legs around me, holding on tight. I wander through the living space and gradually she relaxes her grip. In the bathroom, I sit her on the toilet where she tinkles for a long time. I pull up her panties. In the living room, I lay her on the sofa and cover her with the throw. She is asleep.

I'm wide awake.

I survey the huge room, our stuff scattered here and there. I realize how sloppy and careless I've become. I sweep up the glass from the laundry room floor, gather our trash into a bag, wash and dry the dishes, and put them in the cupboard. I pack everything but Sarah's shorts and sandals in the daypacks and set them in the hallway. If we need to escape, we'll be ready. Prepared for what the dawning day will fling at us, I join Sarah on the sofa and sleep fitfully.

In the morning, I'm electrified by the sound of voices outside the house. I hear a faint metallic scraping from the front entrance and grasp that someone is accessing the realtor lock box.

"Sarah!" I whisper urgently. I read somewhere that lightly pinching the ear lobe will wake a child. She bats irritably at my hand. "Hey, cookie, somebody's coming. Let's go! Laundry room."

She jumps off the sofa and dashes for the hallway, trailing the throw after her. I hastily straighten up the pillows. I grab the trash and snap shut the padlock on the goodies closet. In the laundry room, I boost Sarah through the window, ordering her to wait under the eaves. It's raining and she wraps herself up tight in the throw. Don't blame her, it's cashmere. I drop the daypacks and trash bag next to her.

I hear a woman's voice and footsteps crossing the great room: "This is a marvelous room! Can you believe this view?" Answering murmurs from a man and woman. I softly close the door and climb out the window, shut it silently.

I help Sarah get into her shorts and jacket, and fasten her sandals. I sling both packs on my arms and clutching the garbage bag, we move silently toward the street. Ahead I can hear the purring of a motor. We pause, peeking around the corner. An opulent pearly Cadillac Escalade is parked at the curb with its engine running and windshield wipers whipping back and forth. Two Scottie dogs, one white, one black, are perched with paws scrabbling on the passenger window, adorable noses pressed against the glass, barking as though at an invasion of cats.

I grin in sheer disbelief—the realtor has left her dogs in the heated SUV while she shows the house. Please be unlocked, I pray silently. We scuttle across the yard. I open the passenger door, let the doggies leap out, help Sarah climb into the SUV, dump everything in the back, scoot to the driver's side, release the brake, and ease quietly around the cul-de-sac. In the rearview mirror, I see the dogs zipping around the lawn with joy at their amazing jailbreak.

I roll out onto the street, making a right, then a left, and lose myself in a maze of neighborhoods. After a few minutes, I veer to the curb, move Sarah into the middle row of seats, and fasten her seat belt. She narrows her eyes at me reprovingly.

"Yeah, I get it." I pull a sad face. "Sorry, Sarah." I climb in and wend my way through the neighborhood in the general direction of the Highway 101 strip.

I'd thought it out last night. We're going to revisit Douglas, check out the Osipovich home, and discover the connection between Nichole's father and Beau Cassidy. What do rare, impossibly expensive Fabergé eggs have to do with this story? I want to know. I *have* to know.

We need a vehicle. Cassidy and a representative of law enforcement are aware we're in Florence so I have nothing to lose by withdrawing funds from my bank. I drive the Escalade cautiously. On 101, I locate a branch of my bank and turn into another residential area. I dump the trash in a garbage can by the side of the road. Spotting a cottage with overgrown grass and several newspapers piled on the step, I park in the driveway, leave the keys on the visor, and release Sarah. We walk to the bank.

I withdraw $9,000, chattering to the clerk all about my new used boat and how excited I am to get out on the river. She asks me if I wouldn't rather have a cashier check, and I explain that the boat owner demanded cash. "He's sort of an eccentric old guy." I shrug.

"Have a nice day," she says. "Don't forget your flotation devices!"

If Cassidy and his accomplice have knowledge concerning my accounts and question the teller, they'll presume I'm escaping by water.

We detour to the ladies room, where I separate out seven thousand and tuck it into my jeans pocket. I stow the envelope with the rest of the bills in the bottom of the pack. We traipse along a street paralleling 101. According to my tablet, there's a used car lot six blocks south. Sarah seems to enjoy the rain, pointing at birds, mewing at a fat yellow kitty washing herself on a porch. The rain eases up and we take down our jacket hoods.

At Harry Mann's Used Cars, a nervous young man in a Ducks' ball cap and a Beavers' sweatshirt—ensuring customer approval from both sides of the rivalry?—materializes by my side as we stroll along the row of vehicles. An older fellow in a plaid sports coat and open-necked shirt idles in the door of the office trailer in the middle of the lot, keeping an eagle eye on us. The trailer is festooned with a banner stating, SURPRISINGLY ORDINARY PRICES!

"Hello, there, ma'am!" he cries. "Little guy." He bows to Sarah who stares at him solemnly. "What can I help you with?"

"Are you Harry Mann?"

"No ma'am," he says, doffing his cap to reveal a shaved head. "Not hairy enough!" He chuckles—probably never gets old. "That's Harry." He tips his head toward the other man. "I'm his son Hugh."

"Hugh Mann?" I ask. "Really?"

"Really."

"Alrighty then. Sedan or minivan. Not a Ford, hate Fords. Nothing red – too bright. Low mileage. Maybe a 2005 or '06?"

Hugh Mann ushers us past the cars on offer. "How about a 2006 Corolla?" he asks, Vanna White-ing a champagne

Toyota. "96,000 miles. Priced real low at $9500. Or maybe a Dodge Caravan? It's red, but a pretty dull maroon. 2008. $6999." He glances nervously at the fellow at the office.

"Your dad not too sympathetic?" He bobs a nod, swallowing convulsively.

"Hey, Hugh, it'll be fine," I tell him. "I need a car. You got cars. We'll make a deal, right?" He lights up.

I tilt my head at the Caravan. I like it—it's the Everymom minivan. "Let's drive it."

He trots away, confers with his dad, returns with the key.

Sarah tugs at my elbow. I glance at her—she's scowling.

I sigh. "Um, you got a child seat?"

He beams. "There's one in the van! Isn't that terrific?"

It fits well enough. I strap Sarah in and we motor around the neighborhood. There are no terrible sounds and the Dodge accelerates smoothly. I brake abruptly at several stop signs and the van responds quickly. I try the heat—works fine. I connect to my tablet, review the list of items to beware of in a used car, and don't observe any overt red flags. The van sits level on the pavement on pretty good rubber. The upholstery and carpeting suck—this mustang has been rode hard by a herd of little cowhands. There's a dent in the side panel and another on the tailgate.

Everything that matters is functioning, so I say, "$5200 and you got a deal."

He blanches, glances quickly at the boss. "I can't go that low."

"Did I mention it's cash?"

He leaves and comes back. "Boss says six is as low as he can go."

"Please. For cash? With this crummy interior? Okay, fifty-four, and that's my best offer.

Hugh lopes to the office. Races back. "Fifty-eight."

I pat his arm and smile. "Gosh, I'm sorry. I thought we could come to an agreement. Does Florence have a taxi?"

"Oh no, oh no. Don't go. I'll talk to him." He hustles off again. Sarah and I amble up the street. We're a half-block from the lot when Hugh catches up to us. "Please talk to him," he begs.

I am reluctantly convinced into accompanying him. I give the man at the trailer a steely glare. "Mr. Mann. Fifty-four?"

He takes breath to argue, but then sighs. "Fine."

But when he passes the papers to me to sign, I hesitate and gaze with anxiety at Sarah. "Peanut, would you mind sitting on the steps for a few minutes and decide what to name our minivan?" She obediently goes outside. I can see her through the window.

"You might have noticed my son doesn't talk?" Harry frowns with impatience, eager to seal the deal.

I knock on the window and wave extravagantly. Sarah waves at me with her right arm, her black and blue bruise horribly contrasting with her golden tan.

110

"That's a bad bruise!" exclaims Hugh Mann.

"It's part of why he's lost his words. His daddy hurt him. I'm afraid he'll do worse, that's why I'm getting him to Coos Bay to my mom's."

Harry leans forward. "I hate asshats who beat on their kids. But that's not gonna make me give you the Dodge for less than fifty-four."

"I'll level with you. He'll chase after us. There's an extra thou in it for you if you tell him you haven't seen us."

Harry is shocked. "An extra thou."

"You got it."

"What if your ex offers more?" Jerk.

"He won't. But if he does, you damn well better remember he abused my son. If he finds us, I'll be back to visit you with the sheriff. You'll be an aider and abetter, sure as shootin'." Difficult to say with a straight face.

Hugh says, "Dad, don't be a dick." He's flushed red and sweat beads his forehead. He's glaring at his father with honest outrage. "This is an innocent kid we're talkin' about. You'll be a granddad soon. Shame!" He gazes steadily at me. "Of course we won't rat you out."

Uh-huh. All I can do is hope. If either Mann reveals to Cassidy that we'd fled south to Coos Bay, he'll end up hunting in the wrong direction. I drag the money out of my pocket, and push fifty-four hundred dollar bills toward Harry. And I count out ten more bills and give them to Hugh. We sign papers.

"Nice doing business with you gentlemen."

I strap Sarah into the child seat and drive out onto the Coast Highway, heading south. A few blocks later I cruise the back streets and emerge onto 101 north of Harry Mann Motors. I pause in the lot at Starbucks, connect to check the news.

The news is not good: a witness has stepped forward who'd seen Olive Wiley and Sarah Atkinson together at the Cummins Creek Trailhead parking lot.

Supermom. That bitch.

The item reprises Nichole's death and the report of her missing daughter. Then: "Lt. Colonel Seth Atkinson, Sarah's father, is en route from Iraq. Authorities are now treating the disappearance of Sarah Atkinson, age five, as a kidnapping perpetrated by Lincoln County School District employee Olive Wiley. Wiley is driving a 2003 gray Honda Accord stolen from a house on Shell Beach Road south of Yachats. It is believed Wiley has changed her hair color from blonde to brunette." A computer sketch artist has updated my employee ID photograph. My picture looms on the screen. They have the correct hair color and my photo is disquietingly accurate.

With trepidation, I navigate our minivan north to Douglas.

Despite its clean fifties architecture, Leonid Osipovich's residence has a curious Grimm's fairy tale aura, situated as it is in a dense tangled grove of trees high above the sea. The house is about a half-mile out of town at the end of gravel Grey Whale road, cozied up to the Siuslaw National Forest. The low, modern structure spreads across a broad clearing. Even in afternoon, it is dim under the trees in the overgrown yard. Blackberry brambles strangle the rhodies and the ragged lawn is sere and brown, like many on the coast. Municipal water is expensive, nobody waters.

The nearest neighbor's residence—that of Luanne Green, the woman quoted in the news story about the Osipovich fire, who cares for the dog Carl—isn't visible through the trees. Apparently Osipovich has some acreage. I gawk with dismay at the blackened ruin of the garage adjoining the east end of the domicile. The house windows nearest the garage are covered with raw plywood and scorch marks mar that section of the gray wall. The rest of the residence appears to be untouched by the flames. I drive across the grass and stop the van behind the wrecked garage.

As I get out of the van, the air is saturated with the stench of wet charcoal. I release Sarah from her seat and pick her up. She is rigid in my arms, transfixed by the sight of the house, eyes huge, fist jammed into her mouth. She wriggles like a demented boa, loosing her hold on my neck and sliding down my torso. Landing on her feet, she races for the sliding glass door opening into the interior from a wood deck. I run after her but I'm moving slowly today and barely catch her up as she frantically pounds with determined fists on the glass. Drapes cover the doors and we can't see inside.

"Sarah, wait! Sarah, honey—" I try to lift her but she twists out of my grasp and bolts for another door near the burned end. I catch her before she can reach the dangerous structure, swinging her up and over my shoulder with difficulty. She fights me, pounding my shoulders. I clutch her firmly, making low crooning noises and stroking her hair. An errant elbow smacks me in the nose, making my eyes water. Her mouth gapes wide, as though to call out. No sound emerges, but she is crying 'Mama' with every cell of her body.

I fumble with the side door to the Caravan, sit on the floorboards, and situate her awkwardly on my lap. Her body hums with tension. Sarah lifts her face to me, drowned eyes huge.

"This is your Grandpa's house?" After a pause, she nods.

"Did you expect your mommy would be here? And your doggie?" A barely perceptible nod. Her thumb is in her mouth.

"Sarah, I'm so sorry but your mommy isn't here. No one is here."

She starts to sob and I let her cry it out. When she calms, hiccupping, I wipe her eyes and stretch behind me to retrieve her juice bottle. She drinks thirstily and subsides against my chest. Soon her breathing evens and she is asleep. Interesting how kids fall asleep after they cry. Had I done that when I was a tot?

I slump on the van floor in the quiet woods, my feet resting on the thick layer of pine needles coating the rough grass, wondering how vulnerable we are at Grandpa Osipovich's house. Would Beau Cassidy look for us here? Why would he? To his way of thinking, Olive Wiley would have no knowledge about Leonid Osipovich or anything else about Sarah's family. Therefore, why would he even consider this place as a possible refuge? He would expect that I have taken Sarah for my own inexplicable reasons that have nothing to do with her family.

How about the authorities, would they search for us here? Seems totally unlikely. They'd expect me to run as far as possible. Sooner or later Sarah's father will show up here. That would be good. I believe we are safe for the moment if we stay out of sight. I close my eyes, fatigued from running and changing shelters and seeking information and taking care of Sarah and gnawing at the problem of who murdered Nichole, and how, and why. The more I get to know Sarah, who is a terrific kid, the better I like her mother. I wonder if Nichole and I could have been friends in differing circumstances. Sure, Olive.

Sarah's inability to speak could be due to the trauma of the past days. But what if Cassidy knew Sarah as a chatterbox and assumes she has told me everything that had happened to her and her mother. It pleases me to imagine him puzzled as to why I haven't taken Sarah to the sheriff's department. I hope he's very, very worried. Had the murder taken place here, in this house? If Sarah had informed me of this as a fact, would I have returned to the scene? I feel a great lassitude, from the cancer or the drugs or the stress of making sure Sarah is safe. Even as I realize the danger, I doze off.

Sarah wakes, her bottom wriggling in the got-to-go motion. I have no idea how long we've been sitting here.

"Do you need the bathroom?" She slides to her feet. Kids always have to pee.

As we cross the yard, I stumble and almost fall. Sarah grasps my hand and looks up at me with concern. I smile reassuringly. But I am far from well. And I'm terrified. I can't think or figure out a plan to keep more than one step ahead of Beau Cassidy.

I try the keys on Nichole's key ring. The third fits the lock on the back door, opening into the kitchen. Sarah races through the kitchen and the living room and enters a hallway. Dumping my pack on the floor, I follow and wait for her outside the bathroom while perusing the framed prints lining the walls. They're all signed with a confident scrawl: "Tapies." Sarah slams out of the bathroom and down the hall. She ducks through an open door, tears out, disappears into another, and immediately exits. I examine the rooms: two bedrooms with queen-size beds, furnished in modernist furniture, works of art on the walls. Tasteful and clean. In the third room off the hallway, Sarah scampers up a bunk bed ladder to the top bunk. She perches on the edge, legs dangling.

I survey her decor with interest. "Your room is very cool," I say with admiration.

Her room isn't girlie-girl. No pink, no frills. Three walls are painted lime green, the other turquoise. There are comforters on the mattresses of the white-painted bunks, a contemporary circle pattern, like Ikea. Shelves are filled with books, toys, and stuffed animals. A child-size desk and chair are flanked by storage bins of art supplies. The paintings on the walls are originals, beautiful watercolor studies of sea creatures.

Suddenly Sarah jumps, lands on the furry area rug, executes a perfect somersault, and pops to her feet and out the door. I struggle after her as she urgently beckons me to follow. We cross the living room, furnished with more mid-century classic furniture, some of which I recall from college design history. Surfaces are dusty and the air is chill, smelling of burnt wood and plastic. Sarah struggles with the knob on the French doors, then she is through and slapping at a panel of light switches on the wall. She swirls to a stop before floor-to-ceiling built-in shelves, brightly lit from recessed fixtures.

I stare, astonished. I am viewing a collection of Fabergé eggs ranged evenly on the glass shelves, gleaming with jewels and enamel and gold. Collectively they are incredibly vulgar in their ostentation. Fabulous, outrageous bling.

Sarah is staring at me expectantly. "These are what you were drawing?" Her head bobs *yes* emphatically. She gently strokes the shell of the egg I recognize from my research as the *Romanov Egg.* I approach the shelf. These aren't originals, they can't be. Fabergé eggs are for the most part in museums and private collections, guarded with the highest security.

"Is it all right to touch them?" She nods.

I gingerly pick up the *Romanov Egg* from the shelf. On the bottom, I discern a metal tag containing the name of the manufacturer of Fabergé reproductions, the company with whom Leonid Osipovich had been employed. I count twenty-one eggs on the shelves.

Sarah is humming, fussily moving the eggs on the lowest shelf about and making minute adjustments to their placement. There is now a wide gap between two of the eggs. She knocks gently on the glass.

"Something is missing?" Sarah watches me expectantly. I raise my hands like, *What?*

Sarah whisks out of the room. I wait, too weary to chase the whirlwind. I survey Grandpa Osipovich's study. The other three walls are fitted out with built-in shelves packed with books and journals. A desk and chair occupy the middle of a Persian rug. The desktop is neat: office desk set and landline.

Sarah appears dragging my pack. She rummages in the main compartment, pulling out the sheaf of drawings she'd done during the days before we'd fled Florence. She finds the one she wants and lays it in the gap on the shelf. It is the drawing of the egg with the scrawly, wormy things surrounding it, the egg containing the toiletry tools, similar to the missing treasure called the *Nécessaire*. She's trying to impart that it is missing. But what is 'it?' Another reproduction? But a reproduction isn't possible, as no one has any inkling of what exactly the *Nécessaire* looks like. Perhaps Osipovich had designed and fabricated his own *nécessaire* using the written description to guide him? Or perhaps, as wildly improbable as it is, the vanished egg is genuine.

Sarah tugs on my hand, leading me to the kitchen. She's hungry. I scavenge the extremely well-equipped kitchen. It's odd the refrigerator is stocked with milk, eggs, vegetables, and meat. Then I realize Nichole and Sarah must have been staying here before Nichole's death. I count. Only five days ago, Nichole had been alive, had shopped for food and provisioned her father's refrigerator. Someone in the family had been a skilled cook, the equipment is top-notch. Portland is only three hours from Douglas. The Atkinsons clearly visited Nicholes's father often, maintaining rooms, leaving clothing and possessions.

Sarah perches at the counter, sipping her cup of apple juice. I lay out sandwich makings. "Ham, turkey, or cheese?"

119

Sarah pokes her finger at each of the packages. I put slices of Franz Oregon Trail whole wheat on a plate. Sarah hands me the mustard. I squirt it on, add lettuce, meat and cheese, and cut it into quarters. She nibbles quickly. I can't eat my half sandwich. Sarah finishes and disappears into her room.

I pass through the rooms, closing the drapes tight. I pin towels over the windows in the kitchen to prevent the light from shining out at nighttime. It's chilly but the only heat source is a strange suspended Scandinavian-looking woodstove in the living room. I pass on building a fire. No smoke signals coming out of the chimney. I put on a sweater I find in a closet and dress Sarah in her fleecy.

I try to connect my tablet but there is no Wi-Fi. There is also no television in the house. Was Osipovich a determined Luddite? This is a definite problem. I need to be able to keep current with the news. And sooner or later, I need to contact Sarah's father so that I can return Sarah to him. But I can call or text him on his cell—I have a couple of bars on my cheap burner phone. I feel completely isolated with no data to consider. I'm up here in the woods with no idea what's going on while the rest of the world gyrates around me. What is the progress of the search? Where is Sarah's father? Is he in America yet?

In the meantime, I spend a couple of hours writing a narrative detailing everything I've observed, discovered, and surmised concerning Nichole's death, Beau Cassidy, and Lane County Deputy Camas Cates. I create a file containing the narrative, the downloaded JPGs of the pictures of Nichole's body I'd taken in the cave, the photos of Cassidy with the deputy, and the PDFs of the articles I'd found concerning the Fabergé eggs. Is all my information collected in one tidy package? I'm having a bit of trouble remembering. Reviewing the file, I scold myself. When had I ever had trouble sorting out data? I back up the file onto a flash drive fashioned in the shape of Olaf the Snowman from *Frozen* that I'd picked up at Fred Meyer. Who knew what might happen to me or to my tablet? If the information was with Sarah at least it would be found by her daddy.

I lean in the doorway of Sarah's bedroom, watching her draw.

"Hey, Sarah, I have a present for you." She looks up expectantly. "See? Olaf on a necklace."

She takes the white plastic Olaf figure hanging on its pink lanyard and puts it over her head. She strokes the toy and laughs.

"I'm glad you like it. What are you drawing?"

Sarah shows me a recognizable facsimile of the Osipovich house with a family and a brown dog standing in front. Sarah and her parents, her grandfather and his dog Carl. She industriously colors the dense surrounding trees. I lie on the lower bunk and observe as she busies herself in the sketchbook. I am jealous of her attentive, loving, intelligent mother and brave father, the warm family life she'd experienced, and the comfortable, welcoming homes she lived in. But as desperately as I had yearned for these things as a child, I know this whole mess isn't about me. Returning young Sarah without harm to her family, to her daddy, is the only objective.

Still, the image of a golden egg teases. Thirty-three million dollars.

Of course, my threadbare childhood existence was utterly changed by what Tommy did to me in the men's toilet at the marina. Much later I learned the words *fellatio* and *cunnilingus* by reading a book in the library and thought it unimaginable that people willingly performed these acts for pleasure. After the first time with Tommy, I simply shut my feelings into a locked cupboard in my head. When he let me out of the toilet that night, I crept slowly and carefully to the *Charlie B*, crawled into my sleeping bag on the deck, and laid rigid, listening with dread for Tommy's footsteps on the dock. It wouldn't have occurred to me to confess to my hapless mom and daddy. What good would it do? But Tommy never bothered me on the boat, that night or any other. I wasn't sure if it was because he was afraid of my parents, but I didn't care why. I just wanted him to leave me alone. But I had to get off the boat eventually and when I did, Tommy was inevitably hanging around.

Since then I've heard many stories from the survivors of sexual abuse, all of whom had been asked why they hadn't told someone. There are a wide variety of answers but in my case, Tommy scared me witless, saying he was my parents' dealer and they couldn't or would not do without—so who were they gonna believe? Their daughter or their supplier? Envisioning Charlie and Sean, adrift and angry and in utter despair, I knew exactly whose side they would take. Tommy also promised he would hurt me bad. The warning in his mean green eyes convinced me he'd do it. So I did not tell. Not for the eight months Tommy accosted me on my way from school, or met me in the marina parking lot, or took me out in his truck for a hamburger.

Here was the thing: Tommy provided me with adequate food, I took regular showers and dressed in clean clothes. In spite of being diddled on an almost daily basis, I appeared to be healthier simply because I was fed and clothed. The things Tommy made me do were tucked into my soul, frozen solid, unacknowledged. I studied to keep my mind off those things, earning straight A's though I could barely answer above a whisper in class. I was a third-grader with a secret.

I hadn't imagined my world could get any worse when, on my ninth birthday, Tommy drove me out Bay Road and fucked me on the seat of his pickup. I fought and I screamed like a red fox but he tore into my small body and left me raw and bleeding. Back at the marina, I slammed out of the truck and fled, ran as fast as I could up the hill through freezing sleet, stumbling and slipping and panicking. I glanced over my shoulder. Tommy was chasing after me but he was too far behind and I was much quicker. I ducked into one of my secret byways and easily shook him. I hurt so bad but trod determinedly on, desperately putting one foot in front of the other until I reached the library and collapsed into the alcove by the entrance. I had on a long winter coat Tommy had bought me and it saved my life that winter's night.

I don't remember much but I learned most of it later. In the morning, Miss Goodreade had found me in the alcove, half-frozen, unconscious, my crotch bloody. She'd bundled me into her car and sped to the ER, refusing to move from my side as the doctor and nurse examined me, administered a rape kit, and warmed me up. When I awoke, Miss Goodreade was by my bed smiling into my eyes.

"Everything's fine now, Olive," she said. "You're safe, I promise."

I begged her. "Don't leave me."

"I won't leave you," she declared. I knew she meant it.

Miss Goodreade identified me for the sheriff's deputies. She encouraged me to disclose my rapist's name and what he'd done to me, and so I told. When the law arrived at the marina, there was only a hole where the *Charlie B* had docked and Tommy was AWOL from the

Blue Pacific. My parents had abandoned me, just chugged away into the sunset, probably with Tommy on board. Clearly they had decamped to avoid arrest. No goodbyes, no final hug. On the boat was my history, sparse as it was. My parents' memories had been burnt out by meth and any paperwork encapsulating my miserable biography had vanished, too. The authorities issued bulletins but the boat hadn't docked anywhere. Eventually it was surmised the half-rotten *Charlie B* had gone down at sea with everyone on board.

There was a period after that where I lived with a retired couple, licensed foster parents named Hamilton in an apartment near Walmart. I had a tiny blue-painted room with a quilt Mrs. Hamilton had made spread on the bed. Anna picked me up and took me to school. At 4:00, I walked to the library. After work, she drove me back to the Hamiltons. We would have tea and cookies seated around the kitchen table and then Anna would go home. On the weekends Anna and I visited the aquarium or explored the beach. Sometimes we drove up to Portland to buy books at Powell's or delve into the Portland Art Museum or the Rose Gardens. Sometimes we went shopping. We'd gone to Seattle for four days and we'd had the most awesome time sightseeing, stuffing ourselves with seafood, and riding the ferries to the islands. She'd taken me to the Chihuly Garden and Glass and I'd fallen in love with his multitude of fantastical glass creatures.

By and by, Anna Goodreade officially adopted me. I hugged the Hamiltons bye-bye. I moved into Anna's cozy cottage overlooking the bay and she and I created a haven in our small home.

What is the boundary between despair and contentment? For me it was a matter of contrasts: a man's dirty hand down my panties or a woman's rounded arm cuddling me as we watched a movie; a filthy sleeping bag on a steel deck or a cozy cream-painted room I got to decorate with photos of whales and harbor seals; a Quarter Pounder or oatmeal with fresh peaches for breakfast? Now that I had warmth, food, health care, and the love of someone I adored, I started to speak up in class. I joined the computer club and when the kids saw how curious I was and how fast I learned, they began to share their knowledge: I had peeps. Anna and I volunteered at the Marine Science Center and at Cape Perpetua and even more people entered my life.

But books brought us even closer. We both loved books. We could laze for an afternoon in our living room, a fire crackling in the woodstove, delving into our separate word worlds. Then together we'd make dinner while chattering about our reading experiences. Sometimes we read the same novel. Anna loved mystery novels and those she deemed appropriate, she let me read. As I grew older and chose my own books, it was the subcategory of noir that spoke to me. The grit and darkness, suspense and dread, the notion that for the most part life events don't work out for people–these aspects appealed to me, fit with my worldview. Death, and not necessarily a clean, pleasant, or easy death, awaits us all. My story until age nine had been all noir. Now I lived in a cosy and my biggest fear was it couldn't last.

We had a joyous and peaceful life, and you might expect that everything was all happily ever after. But a tiny shadowed nook of fear remained in my heart. I saw a counselor once a week and told her all about my crappy childhood and the loss of my parents. I also met with a rape survivors group and told the other girls and women about the sexual abuse. This helped. But in spite of all this positive influence—I couldn't explain why, and I knew it would be devastating to Anna if she found out—I couldn't stop stealing.

When living on the *Charlie B*, I'd stolen food and toiletry items to survive but if I was honest, there had also been a thrill in outsmarting adults. Now that my life was so improved, so ineffably secure with a loving friend (it was difficult accepting Anna as my 'mother' as the word had nothing but negative connotations) why the hell couldn't I quit? I didn't reveal my misdemeanors to my therapist, so it took me awhile to work out the reason by myself: I craved the reaction that rose inside me after a theft. I'd be keyed up and anxious before, but afterward I was flying high. Guilt and remorse followed like clockwork. And the whole damn cycle would start up again. Euphoria was the drug.

When I was a freshman, age fourteen, Anna became seriously ill with breast cancer. She fought bravely for a couple of years but when it became clear she wasn't going to beat it, we carefully planned my future. We agreed I would attend a great college and earn a degree in computer science. I had my sights set on Caltech. My grades were top-notch, so if I kept them up throughout high school, I could apply for scholarships. Anna and I also agreed that on my sixteenth birthday we would petition the court so I could be emancipated. I would inherit the cottage and live on her insurance and retirement money. Anna had faith I could be independent, having taught me life survival skills. She also understood that despite counseling I couldn't bear living with anyone else.

I was sixteen when Anna died. I had nursed her with the assistance of hospice care. She grew weaker, emaciated, her skin colorless. She was determined to ingest the least amount of pain medication to maintain lucidity for me, to converse with me, to share our books. I read to her for hours, listening to her labored breathing, her bright eyes fixed on my face. It was both devastating and inspiring to see how tenaciously she fought to stay with me. And I helped her, because I couldn't bear for her to leave me.

But one day as I bathed her skeletal body and treated her bedsores, I came to realize how selfish I was being, how badly she was suffering from physical pain and mental anguish. On the evening of Anna's death, I smoothed her hair and smiled into her eyes. "It's okay, Anna. You can go. I love you and I am strong and I will survive. You can go. I want you to be at peace." She accepted a pain medication patch.

"I love you," Anna whispered. "Be a good human being, Olive."

I sat with her reading *Jane Eyre* out loud. When her breathing ceased I was aware she had gone, but if I stopped I would have to acknowledge my loneliness. I was still reading to Anna when the hospice nurse arrived in the morning.

Even with all our careful planning and hospice counseling, when Anna died I skidded off our carefully planned route into deep water. My grief could not be assuaged. Depression set in. I skipped my appointments with the therapist and meetings with my rape survivors group, I stopped studying. I was out on the beach at all hours and many nights I slept in the dunes in my sleeping bag.

By the time I hit my senior year, my grades had fallen off steeply. I had no chance of a scholarship to Caltech. The school guidance counselor dug up an obscure, odd scholarship to UNLV. I applied for it at the last minute and was awarded the Charlotte and Peter Hastings Scholarship for Orphaned Young Women. I think I got the pity vote—I had been orphaned twice. I moved to Nevada to earn my degree. I did okay academically but became an ace at hacking. Stealing became a high to puncture my loneliness.

This evening in Nichole's father's kitchen, I cook dinner and finally Sarah is able to eat fresh vegetables. The kitchen smells homey, like the snickerdoodles I'm baking in the oven. After dinner, we play *The Ladybug Game* until she tires and yawns. I carry her to bed and read to her for a few minutes; she is asleep. As I stroke her hair, it occurs to me: I've stolen her from Beau Cassidy. The biggest heist, the most delirious high ever.

I sit alone in the dark living room. Thinking about Imperial Eggs, I hatch my plan.

Chapter Seven

I am up early on the morning of the sixth day since Nichole was murdered. Sarah is still asleep. I slept badly, in pain and restless. I'm weaker. I'm out of Vicodin and am now well into the bottle of Oxycontin; a paltry seven tabs remain. This situation must be resolved soon. It's doubtful I can continue to care for Sarah without pain meds.

In Grandad Osipovich's study I settle into his leather chair and let my eyes range about the room. The reproduction eggs glow on the brightly lighted shelves. The bookshelves are crammed with books on art, design, metalsmithing, literature, and travel. A plethora of mineral samples and fossils are arranged in front of the books and my eye is particularly drawn to a magnificent amethyst geode next to a sleek marble sculpture.

I snoop through the paperwork in his desk drawers. Bills, house documents; car, home, health and dental insurance. I peruse a rider concerning coverage of artworks. Wow: Tapies, Constable, Hepworth, a Matisse print, but nothing pertaining to the *Nécessaire*. This list would have been invaluable to me in my former life of crime: swoop in, collect the artworks and provenances, and take off with them. I come across two passports in the name of Leonid Arkadyevich Osipovich. An American citizen, he also has a passport from the United Kingdom. His birth certificate from England is dated 1938. His father, Arkady Borodinich Osipovich, had English citizenship; mother Nichole Alice Haight was American. This is interesting.

In another drawer, I find a batch of grey folders stamped with the logo of the Brooklyn reproduction company who'd employed Leonid Osipovich. Each contains specs for a reproduction egg: instructions, sketches, notes, CAD diagrams, photographs of the finished product. I put the stack of files on my lap and roll over to the display of eggs. One by one, I tally the files with each egg—all complete. No file for the *Nécessaire Egg*.

I survey the office. Where would Osipovich have installed a safe? Gaps have been left between bookshelves to provide hanging space for three teeny, framed landscape paintings. They look English to me, maybe the Lake District? Restrained, lyrical, and lovely—the Constables? I lift them from the wall. There is no sign of a safe underneath. I run my fingers carefully under the shelves, seeking a button to push, a lever to pull.

Nothing. I eye the massive desk positioned in the center of the richly-patterned Persian carpet. Could or would an older man move heavy furniture every time he needed to access a safe in the floor beneath? Highly unlikely. He might have hidden important pages in his books, but I doubt it—fire is the danger. Osipovich would store his important papers in a fireproof container. I search the desk thoroughly for disguised compartments and false drawer bottoms. I detect a cleverly designed secret niche filled with DumDums. Had Leonid and his granddaughter Sarah played a recurring treasure hunting game? But this is the only enigma the desk hides.

I scrutinize the ceiling for an indication of an attic hatch but the pale ochre paint is unbroken. Opening an unobtrusive, narrow door in the corner reveals an orderly closet full of office supplies and plastic storage containers of bills and tax forms. I give the paperwork a cursory read, but the contents are exactly as labeled. I move everything off the closet shelves and scan the walls—they are blank. I detect no evidence of a built-in safe. I'm beginning to suspect Osipovich has a safety deposit box at a bank, but I haven't found a key or record indicating this as a fact. It looks as though I'll have to exert myself to search the rest of the house.

Relaxing in the office chair—garnet leather, sinfully comfortable—I allow the atmosphere of Osipovich's office to seep into my consciousness. An image tugs at the periphery of my mind, an incongruity. I can't coax it to the forefront of my thoughts so I let it drift. It's intriguing that his office, traditional and Old World in mood, is unlike the fifties decor evident in the other rooms. Dark wood, verdant brocade drapes on the window, French doors leading into the living room. The woodwork of the shelving is beautifully done. The desk itself is an antique, maybe 19th century, mahogany with an inset leather top. The mood of the room is restful and elegant, all aspects well-crafted.

I remember Osipovich's profession, the high level of quality, technical ability, and craftsmanship demanded in metalsmithing. Especially craftsmanship. As a master craftsman, Leonid wouldn't have a half-assed hidey-hole. He'd probably designed and built it himself, making sure it was secure. What about his space gives me the impression of being out of place? I consider the *Nécessaire*, the egg Sarah indicated was missing from the glass shelves housing the *Fauxbergés*. Whether it was the real deal or Osipovich's own invention, it had been exhibited in plain sight. Was the concealment of his hidey-hole conceived in a similar vein?

As my eyes rove over the various aspects of the study, they return repeatedly to the closet door. When I'd opened and closed it, the door had felt hefty for such a narrow portal. I examine it more carefully. Yes, it seems thicker than necessary for its width. As I swing it experimentally to and fro it has a feel of solid weight, heavy in relationship to the size. Also mahogany, it has three recessed panels on the outside but is flat on the inside. This is odd in itself as most wooden doors have panels on both sides. I examine the surfaces using Osipovich's magnifying glass. I can't spy a seam or catch enabling me to manipulate any of the panels. The edge upon which the latch is mounted is unbroken. The knob does its job, which is to turn. The hinges are handsome, but only function as hinges. But still there's that puzzling thickness and heaviness . . .

The only section of the door I haven't probed is the top edge. I head back to the kitchen and lug the step stool to the study. Positioning it, I wobble up, steadying myself with a hand on the wall.

And there it is: a brass lever flush with the wood and a dimple where I can insert my finger and pull the lever perpendicular. I tug hard, feeling resistance, then yank harder and a slim steel receptacle slides out of a metal recess neatly fit into the depth of the mahogany. Brilliant.

Grasping the box to my chest, I climb down and carry it to the desk. After unlatching the fastener on the side I raise the lid and remove the contents: aged, fragile pages enclosed in transparent protective sleeves. The first of these leaves me flabbergasted. It is a drawing of a golden egg on a three-legged support. I bring the lamp near and inspect it closely.

The exquisite drawing is rendered in watercolor and ink on pale gray paper with slightly tattered, grubby edges. It is in two parts: one is of a completed egg sitting in its stand; below it, an illustration of the egg separate from its support stand, lying open on its side with its surprises arrayed in an arc.

It is simply labeled "*Nécessaire*" and is signed "*C. Fabergé 1888.*" The fine, sure lines of the master's hand depict the artwork in detail, the gleaming surfaces and jewels painted in color. Fashioned of yellow gold, the egg is completely wrapped with textured, overlapping rose petals and leaves. The large end is set with a sizable diamond and at the other end, a huge sapphire. Scattered across the marvelous texture are rubies and emeralds fitted out as tiny buds. The gold support has been formed from lithe, vine-like rose branches twining together to create a tripod, rising to weave a circle cradling the egg at its widest part. I have been reading a lot about Fabergé eggs and I perceive the style as classic Art Nouveau, fluid and organic, very different from the stiffer more formal eggs created later.

In the second drawing, the egg has been laid on its side, split open on a hinge in the middle, and the contents removed. Slots and holes can be seen in the lower half of the egg, presumably each designed to hold a particular tool. Petite personal hygiene utensils are laid out in an arc on the table, steel toiletry implements with gold handles echoing the roses and leaves theme, encrusted with diamonds. Thirteen instruments, just as reported. Several I cannot identify, but I recognize tweezers, penknife, scissors, fingernail buffer, knife, nail file, teeny spoon—an ear scraper?—and a slim tubular crystal bottle.

I am suspicious; Osipovich could have forged the drawings himself. Visually, however, these lovely drawings match the description of the *Nécessaire* on the Fabergé Research Site saved on my tablet.

I review the article once again. In 1949, an exhibition of Fabergé artworks had been held at Wartski, in London. This was the very same gallery who in 2012 had partnered with one very lucky Midwest scrap dealer in selling the *Third Imperial Easter Egg* he'd found in a flea market. Interesting.

Recently, a staff member at Wartski named Kieran McCarthy had done a great deal of research into the 1949 exhibition and discovered that an egg in the form of an *etui* had been exhibited. The piece had been loaned anonymously, so its antecedents were unknown. By combing through Russian archives, McCarthy found the *Nécessaire Egg* listed in the ledgers, along with a description. Sure enough, this egg had been sold by the Soviet state. Using these records, he was able to connect the *Nécessaire* description to that of the egg displayed in the 1949 Wartsky exhibition. The *Nécessaire* was by no means the star of the show; the only photograph of it from this exhibition was a blurred image of the end of the egg—partly obscured by a piece of fabric—on a display shelf close to the floor. At the time, this was the sole visual record of the *Nécessaire* known to exist.

Wartski's records also showed that the egg had been sold in 1952 and that the buyer had insisted on anonymity. This was the last time the *Nécessaire Egg* was recorded as having been seen. McCarthy's research had come to a dead end.

But my research is more rewarding. The next plastic-encased page found in the metal box almost convinces me that Osipovich had had the original *Nécessaire* in his possession. It is a bill of sale, the cream colored paper folded and worn, with the letterpressed Wartski logo and address at the top. The wording, written in exquisite penmanship, is identical to the history of the egg online:

Carl Fabergé, Nécessaire Egg, *1889, St. Petersburg, Russia. An* etui *made of gold, diamonds, sapphire, rubies, and emeralds opening to reveal a thirteen-piece set of toiletry instruments set with diamonds.* The date is 1952. The buyer is described as "A Stranger".

The next sheet appears to have been torn from a diary. The printed date is "13 iyunya 1948." The page is crowded with dense writing in what I believe is Russian Cyrillic script. On the back is a typewritten

English language document dated 1966. The headline states: "This is a translation of a record drafted by my father accompanying the *Nécessaire Egg*." Signed Leonid Osipovich.

Eagerly, I skim the translation and learn that Leonid Osipovich's father—Arkady Borodinich Osipovich—had been the workmaster for the construction of the Fabergé *Nécessaire Egg* in 1888. The egg had been presented to the Tsar in 1889. After the Revolution, Arkady had escaped Russia and made his way to France where he tried to assist Fabergé's sons with a resurgence of the family business. After this proved to be unsuccessful, he'd been employed for seventeen years at Cartier, then had emigrated to England and became employed at the Victoria and Albert Museum as a restorer.

Despite their age difference, he'd married a young curator in the fashion collection in the museum, Nichole Haight, an American. They'd had a son, Leonid, then three more children. Virile guy into his eighties, Arkady Borodinich. He'd been indefatigable in tracking the whereabouts of his fellow metalsmiths of the team from the Fabergé workshop in Russia— they'd most likely been scattered all over Europe—and in 1952 they'd established a consortium to purchase the *Nécessaire* from Wartski. The seven metalsmiths agreed to a tontine, in which the final survivor would inherit the treasure. That hearty old bastard Arkady Borodinich

Osipovich had been the last man standing. His heir, his son Leonid, also a metalsmith, had eventually smuggled the *Nécessaire Egg* to America.

The final document is most likely the tontine agreement, penned by hand in Russian with indigo ink. Seven spidery signatures sprawl across the bottom of the page. I contemplate what the tontine had meant to these craftsmen. Their work had been vilified by the new government after the Revolution. The Imperial Eggs had been sold for a song to institutions and people around the world. As artisans, they had been forced to either seek a different kind of work or leave Russia behind. The teamwork required in constructing something as beautiful as the *Nécessaire* had surely been a profound and authentic artistic experience. Emotions about the partnership would have run deep. Clearly, after the sacrifice and effort of recovering and owning the egg, caring for the treasure had been an almost sacred trust for the son, Leonid. This expectation must have been passed to his daughter Nichole whose professional commitment was to preserving the artworks of the past. Selling the *Nécessaire* would have been unthinkable in this family. I assume the discovery of the theft of this artifact had been almost unbearable to Nichole.

I realize that I am convinced of the truth of the story told by these records. If authentic, these documents, so artfully concealed, provide an excellent provenance for the lost egg. I surmise that the *Nécessaire Egg* had been camouflaged among the copies and had consequently been stolen by Beau Cassidy while inspecting the domicile after the garage fire.

But why had Cassidy chosen that particular egg, out of all the brilliant facsimiles on the well-lighted shelves? This had all the hallmarks of terrible luck for Nichole; many of the reproductions were flashier, thus seeming more valuable to the uninitiated, than the *Nécessaire*. I examine Cassidy's choice from a thief's point of view: for one thing, it was smaller, able to be easily accommodated in the capacious pockets of Cassidy's firefighter pants. Perhaps he had even had the time to examine the underside of each egg and pilfered the only one not marked as a reproduction. As a pawnbroker's son, he would have discerned the ornament was gold. The *Nécessaire* was without the colored enamel found on most of the eggs and would have been easier to melt down to sell for the value of the gold.

If he had already busted up the treasure, he'd made a colossal $33 million mistake. I fervently hoped he had stayed his hand.

After the theft, what chain of events had led to his murdering Nichole and her child? I surmised that when Nichole had driven to Douglas after the fire, she'd immediately noticed the loss of the *Nécessaire*. What a horrible discovery it must have been for her, the stress

141

level stratospheric. Her father had died of drowning and/ or a heart attack in a weird car accident; then the house had caught on fire and her father's dog was almost killed; and last, the *Nécessaire* had been stolen. Nichole would have been out of her mind with worry and grief, unable to turn to her absent husband for help or comfort.

But after finding out the identity of the firefighter who had saved her father's dog, she had a viable suspect, a man who had been present at the fire with the opportunity to steal the artwork. Would she have reported the loss to the department chief? The insurance company? The sheriff's department? Or would she have questioned or confronted Cassidy on her own? I assume the latter—after all, her family had kept the ownership of the *Nécessaire* secret for the past sixty-four years. Nichole clearly had her own reasons for continuing to do so.

I tuck the documents back inside and carefully return the steel box to its hiding place in the closet door.

I set my plan into motion by calling Beau Cassidy on the burner cell.

He answers, sounding alert and brisk. "Cassidy here."

In a low, mellow voice, I say, "Hello, Beau. This is Olive."

Silence on the line, then, "What the fuck?"

"You heard me."

Cassidy, sounding taken aback, sputters, "I don't believe . . . who is this?"

"Excuse me, Beau," I say sweetly. "I didn't realize you are hard of hearing. OLIVE WILEY."

"Are you fucking kidding me? Everybody's looking for you and the kid you kidnapped." He is incredulous.

"Aw, Beau, c'mon. You and I know what happened to Nichole and Sarah Atkinson." Cassidy mutters something unintelligible. I prompt him: "You need to speak up, Beau."

"Where are you? How's the girl? *Where's* the girl?" Urgency in his voice.

"We need to talk, Beau."

Cassidy bluffs it out: "Where are you, bitch?"

"Temper, temper. I need you to listen closely. Are you listening, Beau? During the fire at the Osipovich house, you stole a golden egg. You killed Nichole and abandoned Sarah to drown in the sea cave."

Cassidy blusters, "Fuck you. I didn't—"

"Manners, Beau. I want to make this clear for you: all my evidence has been documented and sent to a trusted associate. If I don't check in at regular intervals, the file will be sent to the authorities: sheriff, state police, FBI, newspapers—you name it."

This, of course, is a blatant lie. I can't see any advantage to actually sending the stuff to QC. I only need to convince Beau that I have precautions in place.

"What the . . . ? Again—fuck you."

I speak soothingly, reasonably. "Beau, Beau, use your head. There's no reason for you to be distressed.

Our partnership should be pleasant and mutually profitable."

"What partnership?" he demands.

"Why, the one you and I are forming, the one in which we'll make a ton of money. We will meet civilly and peacefully. You'll come alone and unarmed. You will tell no one where you are going. If I see an inkling of something I don't like, the data gets released. If you aren't super polite to me, the data gets released. Do you understand?"

"Where?" he barks.

"The Osipovich house."

"Are you fucking kidding me?" His voice rises, cracking.

I laugh at him and continue. "Ten o'clock tonight. You will be alone and without a weapon. Don't even think about creeping the property or coming early—I've got excellent surveillance. Park your truck behind the house and strip to your underwear before you approach the front door. Can you remember this? Anything I don't like, the information gets released."

I cut the connection.

Of course I've also lied about surveillance on the property. All I'd done is spread bubble wrap under the windows and inside the doors. At least this flimsy protection will warn me if someone tries to enter the house besides Beau.

It is almost Sarah's bedtime. I concoct a special smoothie for her dessert, peach with lemon yogurt, orange juice, ginger ale, and a crushed up Benadryl. She loves it and drinks it eagerly. After watching her brush her teeth, I get her into her jammies. I sit with her comfortably ensconced in my arms and read *The Paper Bag Princess* until her eyelids droop and she is fast asleep. I watch her for a time, thinking how much this little girl has come to mean to me, how tender my feelings and how fierce my desire to protect her. Easing out from under her, I make my preparations.

In Leonid's bedroom, I clear the floor of the walk-in closet by moving shoes and boxes onto the shelves. I raid the other bedrooms for blankets and quilts, arranging them on the carpet to build up a comfy mattress, piling the end high with cushions and pillows. I plug in a small reading lamp and place it where it can't touch hanging clothing. Bringing selected stuffed animals from Sarah's room, I tuck them beside the makeshift bed in the miniature den. I put a framed photograph of Sarah with her smiling parents and the plastic box of Tic Tacs atop a stack of her favorite books. Add a bottle of water and a plate of cookies. There. All cozy.

Gently picking Sarah up, I transfer her into her cubbyhole. I'm weaker—it's taking much more effort for me to lift her. I lower her to the thick pad of comforters and spread the cashmere throw over her. I slip a hand into her pj's to ensure she's wearing the Olaf flash drive pendant and kneel for several minutes, memorizing her dear sleeping face. I survey the little sanctuary: it's comfy and warm, suffused with soft light. Her cherished things are surrounding her, so if she should awaken she won't be scared. But according to the internet, she will not wake up til morning; an adult Benadryl tablet is a powerful sedative for a child her age. I kiss her gently, rise, close the door, and turn out the bedroom lights. I make the bed and hang up clothes in her room. Inspecting the house, I tidy away anything indicating the presence of a child.

In Nichole's bathroom, I brush my teeth and use mouthwash; bathe, shave, and care for my neglected nails. I moisturize with Nichole's La Mer. She bought expensive products and obviously cared about her appearance, but most likely she hadn't slathered the unbelievably expensive La Mer all over her body. I normally hate perfume but a bottle with the label *Musc Ravageur* appeals to me. I dab a bit on my pulse points. Use her blow dryer to tousle my dark hair into a flirtatious do. I raid Nichole's cosmetics stash and do a quick mani-pedi, polishing my nails with scarlet enamel. Tending to my makeup with extra attention, I use Nichole's concealer to erase the dark shadows under my eyes, foundation and

146

blush to brighten my pallor, add shadow and mascara, and draw Adele cateyes with eyeliner. I sniff my wrist. The perfume has blended with my chemistry and I smell divine, musky and sensuous. I smooth on Kat Von D lipstick in Poison Apple.

War paint.

I don my armor. Nichole had been taller but I dig up a pair of sleek black leggings and a skintight low-cut top—both fit well enough. A Wonderbra boosts the girls up to new heights, making my décolletage indeed wondrous. I am taller in high-heeled booties, my legs long and sleek. Nichole's diamond studs sparkle in my ears.

I study my reflection in the full-length mirror, mentally transforming my sick, tired carcass into my chosen persona. I am no longer faced with Olive Wiley— ill, Patagonia-clad Northwest beach bum—but rather, a slim, elegant ninja with huge blue eyes sparkling with mischief, wide red mouth, sensual figure, and an air of confidence and humor. These are the weapons I take into battle with Beau Cassidy.

It's 9:30. I go out into the yard. If I don't survive this night, this will be the last evening I'll experience Venus rising above the horizon, a diamond-sharp beacon in the ultramarine sky. I shake my head ruefully. You've already been there and done that, Olive. I close my eyes and inhale deeply. The scents of Oregon are of the sea, fir bark, and the fresh green smell of the dense vegetation on the floor of the forest. The wind has risen and blows through the tall Douglas fir, a gentle vast breath. I hear the distant roar of big surf bashing the beach far below. I ache to be down by the water, out of harm's way in Wiley Cave.

Chapter Eight

I await Beau Cassidy in the dim living room of Leonid Osipovich's house, alone with my thoughts and plans as Sarah sleeps deeply, hidden and safe. Since I was raped in a Ford F-150 pickup truck, I've never been taken by another person, either in the sense of sexual penetration or that of being conned. But I have used my miserable childhood experiences with my daddy's dealer. I've parleyed those grapplings into a series of techniques to get my way from any heterosexual male—to trick, take, con, wheedle, and steal. I'm an expert at sex up to the point of the final act when it stops being a game, and fear and nausea glut my body. I am the queen of foreplay, the mistress of anticipation.

Therefore, I know Beau Cassidy. I know what makes him tick. He loves beautiful women. I wager he's into straight sex, relishes the seduction. But I speculate on the hidden presence of another side to Beau, one that the straight-up, beer-guzzling, selfless firefighter would not necessarily be in touch with. Judging from the carelessness with which the bodies—one dead, one alive—were dumped in the cave, I conclude that Beau has a burgeoning appetite for violence. I think it started with the theft of the egg, clearing the way for him to dip his toe into the pool of corruption. His relationship with Camas Cates—whom I suspect of a malign influence on our boy—extended from the theft. It's just a presentiment, but I will know when I meet him, talk with him, smell him. I'll know how to get my way. I'll convince Beau to wade in a bit deeper. If I'm successful, he'll drown in the murky, cold depths.

When Beau appears, he isn't wearing shorts. He's stark naked.

Striding through the unlocked door with easy grace, he stands posed, long legs spread apart, fists on narrow hips: Superman. His confidence is well-deserved. His body is taut and muscled, broad at the shoulders, theatrically back-lit by the porch light. I don't delight in the male package but I judge his equipment as more than adequate.

I'm coiled into a corner of a Swedish-modern sofa, an odd chartreuse color. I've piled up cushions to soften the hard-edged upholstery. Soft illumination emits from a Tubino lamp on the table by my side. The rest of the room is unlit.

"I see you've come unarmed," I look him up and down with appreciation, "but not exactly without a weapon."

Beau gives a curt guffaw and nods with contempt at my pink Beretta. "That toy's not gonna do you much good."

I smile. "She shoots the same bullets as her big brothers. But I suspect I won't need her after you hear what I have to say. Turn all the way around." I sketch a circle with the end of the barrel. Beau lifts his arms, rotates a slow three-sixty, grinning over his shoulder. His back is as excellent as his front. I let slip a small smile of homage.

I toss him the throw from the sofa. "Cover up before you embarrass yourself." I am flirting a little, my face relaxed and amused. He picks up the blanket and knots it about his waist.

I indicate an Eames armchair with a small movement of the pistol. "Sit," I order.

Beau snickers, throws his head back, and howls like a dog, "Owooooo."

He settles into the low-slung leather chair and it makes a *whoof*. He places his arms on the curved arms and swivels back and forth, finally comes to a rest, knees spread wide.

We regard each other.

"You're not what I expected," Beau says.

"Oh? Why is that?"

"Driver's license picture sucks. Had no idea you were such a babe."

"Babe," I repeat with amusement.

"Yep." He surveys me judiciously. This is his *Jeopardy!* area of expertise. "Where's the girl?"

"Ah, foreplay done with?"

His gaze is on my breasts. "For now."

"Sarah is safe with friends."

A spasm of annoyance passes over his face. "How'd I miss you in Florence?"

"I was way ahead of you, Beau. Where's your partner?"

Beau is taken aback. "What partner?" Clearly he wasn't expecting this.

"Deputy Camas Cates."

Visibly thrown, Beau blusters, stalling.

"Don't," I warn him. "We're beyond this kind of lying. Where is she? Waiting out in your truck? Sneaking in the kitchen door?"

"I took you seriously about that evidence you talked about. I came alone. She has no clue I'm here."

I'm skeptical. "Can't say I believe that. But if you brought her, you're dead. I don't like you much and I won't hesitate to shoot."

"I'm by myself," he insists.

"Wonderful." I beam at him. "We have a lot to discuss."

"What has the kid told you?" He's apprehensive.

"Well, Beau, that's the thing. You lucked out. She can't talk, she can't write."

"What do you mean she can't talk? She talks."

"Maybe you and Camas scared the holy crap out of her. But she doesn't speak now."

"Then how the hell did you find out about me and Camas?"

"Reasoning. Data. Not a difficult story to figure out."

Another thing occurs to him and he switches tracks. "What were you doing in the cave?"

"Personal reasons, Beau."

He props his elbows on his knees, looks askance at me. "Why didn't you drown? Follow us out of the cave?"

"It was too late. We got up on a ledge."

"Ah." The short word is tinged with regret. If only we'd both drowned, life would be so easy. He eases back in his chair.

"Start at the beginning," I suggest. "I get that it was tempting to encounter a wall of pretty trinkets in a burning house . . ." Beau doesn't respond. "All of us could use more money. I get *why* you stole an egg. But why choose that particular one?"

"What egg?"

"Beau, cut it out." I'm casual, smiling. "I've gathered all the pertinent information for my colleague to release the file. Let me enumerate the evidence for you . . ." I take him through the trail of proof that I have compiled, including the photographs of Nichole's dead body and the picture of his meeting with Camas Cates in front of the mom 'n' pop motel in Florence. "You really need to grasp this: you are fucked. I'm going to offer you a way out, but you need to fill in some blanks before I decide what to do with you."

Beau narrows his eyes, stares intently at my face, clearly trying to determine if I'm telling the truth. He's sort of a simple guy—I can hear the gears grinding. I might have to repeat myself before he gets it.

"So again, Beau, what made you choose that particular egg?"

He glances at me with superiority. "It was gold, real gold. I've worked for my dad, recognize it anywhere. It fit right into my pocket. Returned to the station and sneaked it out to my truck."

"Are you in the habit of stealing stuff from homes? After a disaster when you guys are traipsing in and out?"

"Naw. Most folks don't have nothing worth stealing. But I'd had a super disgusting experience with the dog and I was in the mood for a reward." Beau shrugs. "Didn't really think it through."

He didn't really think it through—I've got him. I ask, "And what were you going to do with this golden egg?"

"Take it up to my dad's pawn shop in Astoria. Yank the gems out of their mounts for appraisal, then melt it for the gold."

I close my eyes. "And did you do that, Beau? Take it to your dad's?"

"Nope. Haven't had any consecutive days off."

I open my eyes wide, let him see me draw in a huge breath of relief. "You fucking idiot. Do you have any clue as to the value of the damn thing?"

Beau uneasily shifts his weight, leather squeaking. "It's valuable?"

"More money than you can imagine."

I pick up my tablet, the document describing the *Nécessaire* on the screen, and frisbee it to him with contempt. He catches it in his mitt of a hand.

"This is what you stole," I inform him. "It's worth millions."

Beau reads. It takes awhile, then he stills. "Are you sure? What about all the other eggs?"

"The others are reproductions—essentially worthless. But I discovered the provenance on the egg you stole. I'm positive it's original, the one described in the article."

"What's *provenance*?"

"A history, the paperwork from the day the *Nécessaire* was created in the 19th century up to the present. It's the real deal."

"Let me have a look at those papers," Beau demands.

"You don't get it, do you?" I say with exaggerated patience. "Do you think I would leave a single piece of information for you and your girlfriend to discover? You really need to listen to me: everything—the provenance, the evidence of murder, the photographs—has been sent to a certain third party. Understand, Beau, you're screwed unless my contact hears from me by—well, by the time I have specified."

He grins. "Maybe. But I've still got the egg."

"This is true." I pause for a beat. "Look, we're at a stalemate. But I don't really want all that incriminating data to be sent to the law. I want in—a partnership, Beau. You and me. You will see that it's the only way forward for you."

Beau is silent, his face troubled.

I move a bit nearer to Beau. "Look, we're going to discuss the terms of our partnership in selling this incredibly valuable object. But first I need data. What's the latest on the search for Sarah and me?"

He looks up. "It's intense. Tons of cops on the lookout for you on the south coast, down around Coos Bay. Cops all over the state are on the alert. You kidnapped a *child!*" The hypocritical asshole has the gall to sound outraged. "There are constant media appeals to citizens to turn you in—they set up a special number for anyone with information. They found out you bought a minivan and the description's being broadcast. That's why the search moved down to Coos Bay."

So Harry and Hugh Mann did sell me out—no big surprise. I ask, "Where's Sarah's daddy?"

"The military had some problem extracting him out of Iraq. He's flying in tonight or in the morning."

"And the autopsy on Nichole? What did they find?"

"Head injury. The ME said Mrs. Atkinson was a victim of homicide. Everybody wants to know why you murdered her and took her kid. So when Atkinson gets into town? Wife dead, kid abducted?" Beau chuckles. "The man will be baying for your blood."

156

"Wait a minute. How was the ME able to determine she was murdered?"

"He found the taser marks."

"What taser marks?" I inquire.

Beau is silent.

"You guys tased her? But then why the hell kill her? Seems like a terrible mistake."

Beau snorts. "I didn't. That was Camas."

"Oh, please." Maximum sarcasm.

"Camas killed her. But it wasn't on purpose."

"Where and how?"

Beau sighs. "When Mrs. Atkinson came down from Portland with her daughter to inspect her dad's home after the fire, she noticed the egg was missing and went down to the station to talk to Chief Ponsler."

I nod encouragingly.

"She brought the dog and her kid along to visit me, like we had some special relationship. Thanked us for saving the house and the mutt." Beau smiles ruefully. "That Sarah could not stop babbling about how she loved the dog Carl and she couldn't have stood it if anything bad had happened to him, blah, blah, blah. She thanked me over and over. She hugged me and wouldn't let go."

"Heartwarming." My tone is dry.

He sends me a look of doubt. "Sarah was definitely a chatterbox. And now you say she can't talk?"

I shake my head.

Beau continues, "Mrs. Atkinson demanded to talk to the chief in private. After awhile he called me into his office while the volunteers watched Sarah, letting her climb up on the engine. Chief asked who had cleared the domicile. He had the paperwork on his desk so he knew the answer but I reminded him of who had responded. He asked me straight up if I had stolen anything and I swore I hadn't."

"You're a great liar."

Beau regards me with interest. "You, too, I bet. Takes a liar to recognize one."

I shrug. "Then what?"

"He dismissed me. I assume he spoke to the volunteers who'd been there. Beats me why Mrs. Atkinson believed them and not me, but she phoned the next day requesting that I come by her dad's house. I was supposed to drop the rescue unit at the dealership for servicing but instead drove it to the Osipovich house."

"And you took Camas with you?"

"She's my girlfriend, she knew all about the fire and the gold egg. She wore her uniform to make Mrs. Atkinson feel secure."

"That was smart," I say admiringly. "And what happened at that meeting?"

"It went bad fast. Mrs. Atkinson was furious, met us on the steps yelling that she was sure I was the thief. She said if I brought the egg back she wouldn't push the issue any farther, no complaint filed. Camas was calm, like deputies are? She had us sit at the kitchen counter like a cop mediating a tense situation. Mrs. Atkinson simmered down. Camas questioned her first, then me. I swore I hadn't taken the egg. Atkinson lost it again, shouting that I was the logical thief and that Deputy Cates should arrest me then and there. Camas tried to shush her but Mrs. Atkinson jumped up and rushed to the counter by the stove where she'd left her phone. She was reaching for it when Camas tased her in the shoulder. She dropped like a sack of concrete. And that's when things got worse."

"Worse?" I echo.

Beau bends forward, studies his bare feet. "When Atkinson fell, she hit her temple on the granite counter and was knocked unconscious. Then that Sarah flew into the room, screeching at the top of her lungs. Camas was gonna shock her but I swung the kid out of the way. She was screaming and Camas was yelling so I just carried Sarah to a bedroom, locked the door, and held onto her. Camas was out of control."

I am incredulous. "Jesus Christ, Beau. Is she crazy? What happened next?"

"I'm great with kids. I explained I was a sort of doctor and I knew what to do to wake her mommy up, but she had to be a good girl. She eventually calmed down and I said to wait there while I cared for her mommy. She curled up on the bed. She was in shock."

He's great with kids. I show no reaction to his narrative, motioning with the Beretta Nano for him to continue.

"Camas and me loaded Mrs. Atkinson on the gurney and into the unit. She was dead by then. Since Sarah was so upset, I told Camas to put on a fire department slicker and climb into the driver's seat, ready to motor. I mixed up a couple of Benadryl in a bottle of juice and the kid drank it. I carried her out and buckled her up in the back. She was super concerned about her mom, kept attempting to crawl out of the seatbelt. But then she conked out."

I wriggle in my corner of the sofa—I've gradually worked my way close to him—and smirk mockingly at him. "You are so full of shit."

"What?" Beau eyes are wide and innocent.

"Fell and hit her head? Really? You watch TV, Beau. Perps in cop shows always claim they haven't murdered anybody, the dead guy merely slipped and conked his head on the bathtub or the fireplace. Such a cliché. How many human beings actually die that way?"

"Surprisingly many in my experience." Beau is defensive.

"Still, you're lying. Maybe you hit her while she was out?"

"No! Camas tased her. But then—" Beau pauses, biting his lip.

"Then . . . ?" I prompt.

"Then Camas kicked her."

"Kicked her?"

"Kicked her in the head. Hard, with her steel-toed shoes. I grabbed Camas and jerked her back from Mrs. Atkinson before she could do it again. Camas said don't worry, we'll make it look like an accident."

"Wishful thinking."

"You think? Camas was scaring me big-time."

"Why is that?"

"Deputy Camas Cates is tough and has a mean streak. She always wanted to be a cop growing up, likes being in power, loves wearing a gun. She has to be respected, likes it better if people are afraid of her. She's a spoiled rich girl who never earned anything herself except becoming a cop. The job suits her. She's got the sheriff wrapped around her little finger."

"Where did you meet?"

"In a bar. She's gorgeous. On duty, pins her hair in a bun, no makeup. But that night at the Flounder Inn, she was really something. Hair loose, sexy dress, great body. God—mind-blowing sex."

"How long have you been an item?"

"Six months or so." Beau is unenthused.

"Sex not so mind-blowing now?" Sardonic.

Beau uncrossed his arms, rubbed his palms on his thighs. "It's okay. But Camas has been wound pretty tight. She's been a bitch on wheels since Mrs. Atkinson."

I pout at him. "Poor baby." Then, "Why leave them in the cave?"

Beau said, "Camas's idea. We get hundreds of calls reporting stupid accidents, clueless tourists getting themselves in major trouble on the coast. I guess it keeps us in business. We decided to set it up like they'd been trapped in the cave at high tide. Mrs. Atkinson's body would be all bashed up on the rocks. Medical examiner wouldn't be able find out for sure the cause of death, if or when the bodies were found. They might stay in there or float out to sea. And the cave's down the coast from Douglas. Camas said that was important."

"Weren't you afraid the rescue unit would be spotted at the wayside?"

"We were only there a few minutes. We hid the Atkinsons in the dunes and hightailed it out of there. I dropped Camas at my place. I took the rig to the dealership and left it parked in the lot to be serviced the next day. She'd followed me in my pickup and we returned to the beach. Inflated my dingy. Loaded up the girls and towed them through the surf to the cave and dumped them out."

"You had your department slickers on."

He surveys me, curious. "Yeah. Why?"

The whole case began with my recognizing their jackets with the **DOUGLAS** logo. Would this story have evolved differently if they'd been wearing anonymous jackets? Of course—I would have taken Sarah down the beach and turned her over to the sheriff's deputies when they recovered her mother's body.

"Never mind. Why'd you leave Sarah alive?"

"Camas had offed Mrs. Atkinson. I figured if the kid was alive, at least I wasn't guilty of homicide." There was a pause. "We didn't talk about it."

"And Nichole's SUV?"

"Camas drove Mrs. Atkinson's Toyota up the logging roads and we abandoned it on an overgrown track."

"You lucked out, Beau Cassidy. It sounds like you're innocent, at least of homicide."

I pat the cushion of the sofa. "Hey, why don't you sit by me?"

Rising, Beau pads to the sofa and warily perches upright beside me on the stiff upholstery, arms folded defensively. I lean toward him with an expression of intense interest, giving him time to further sense my scent and the warmth of my body.

"Then what did you do?"

He stares at me with a bewildered expression on his face, but rouses himself to continue: "Camas was on duty in Florence in the a.m. so she split. I slept. In the morning the report came in from the surfers and I was called out for the recovery. We trailered the jet skis to the wayside and hauled the corpse out of the water. There was no sign of the kid."

I hum sympathetically and edge closer. Beau smells of male sweat and antibacterial soap. I catch a whiff of sausage pizza on his breath, and beer.

Beau turns toward me. "I wasn't worried about the kid not being found," he continues. "It's a real big ocean. But there was that Subaru in the parking lot. Nobody walked up from the beach to claim it—the beach was deserted. The hood was cold and the windows completely covered with dew. Deputies figured it must have been there all night. It was important to talk to the owner— to you—and find out if you knew anything about the victim. Ran your name with the plate number and tried your cell. Sheriff sent an officer to your condo—no one there. Two of us volunteered to search the beach. We split up and it was sheer luck I chose south. There were no footprints on the beach but there were a slew of scratch marks in the sand, leading from inside the empty cave to the water. Tide was coming in. I waded around the rocky ridge to the next beach. Nobody in sight, no prints. You did a helluva job getting the kid out of there. Back at the wayside I informed the deputies there was no sign of anybody. I returned the rig to the firehouse, unhitched the trailer with the jet skis, and drove to the neighborhood south of the cave. Were you in that house the first time I was there?"

I smile, refusing to be drawn, asking, "So after the authorities identified the victim, weren't you questioned? The chief must have connected Nichole's homicide with her reporting the theft of the egg. Why aren't you the prime suspect?"

"Yeah, of course they interviewed me. But that's the cool advantage of having a girlfriend who's a cop. She swore I was with her all night at her apartment in Florence."

"And of course the Lincoln County Sheriff's Department believed a deputy from a neighboring county."

"Yup."

My mind is whirring. I slither close to Beau and lay my hand flat on his smooth muscular chest, feel his heart beat. He is warm and intensely alive. "Why aren't you cold?"

"I'm never cold." Beau's eyes seek mine. "So now what?"

I lightly play my fingers down his chest to his flat stomach, tracing the muscles gently, letting my eyes linger on his six-pack. Then I give him a callous slap. Laughing, I say, "It's up to you, Beau. You're in a world of trouble. Not sure what to advise you."

Beau grabs my hand and rubs his thumb over my wrist. "What's this partnership you propose?"

I snatch my hand away and raise the Beretta with the other. "I thought we could work something out. But now with what I've learned about Camas?—I don't think so. She's a liability, sounds like a psychopath. I mean, what kind of law enforcement officer boots an unconscious woman?" My words are tinged with bitterness—easy, Olive.

I say cheerfully, "Nope, if Camas is part of this deal, I'll just hang out here with you until my colleague sends out the evidence file. What law enforcement agency do you think will show up first?"

Quick as a closing anemone in a tide pool, he's wrapped his arms around me tight enough to hurt. "Tell me what I should do. What do I have to do to get you to call off your evidence guy?"

I laugh up at him. "Ah, this what you like, Beau? Rough stuff?" I glance at his lap, where the throw has burgeoned into a tower. The gun drifts up over my thigh and I caress his erection with the barrel.

Alarmed, he exclaims, "Get that thing away from me." Shoving me from him, he retreats to his end of the sofa, sulking.

I deposit the Beretta deliberately on the end table. I walk on my knees across the sofa to Beau, strip off the blanket, and straddle him, gripping his legs with mine, fondling his cock, tucking it under my crotch, lowering my weight and grinding against him. I put my hands behind his neck, pull him forward, kiss his lips, then bite sharply. Beau rears back, staring, bleeding, then lurches forward and kisses me hard. His blood is slippery, tastes salty. His strong hands are gripping me, hurting me. But I know what I'm doing.

I ease up, gently move against him. "That's better," I gasp, my tongue licking his blood from my lips. He kisses me again and I melt against his chest. He tightens his embrace and I pull away a little, looking intently into his eyes.

166

"Beau, wait just a second. Listen. I know how to broker a deal with someone who has the clients who can afford the egg." My tongue teases his ear, his pulse, lingers on his neck, tastes his bitter sweat.

I murmur, "With an artwork this rare, we have to approach very carefully. We speak of this to no one, understand? If it brings $33 million, our share will be most of it, even after the broker's commission."

I ride him harder now. His breathing quickens, his hands are urgent on my breasts. He tugs at the waistband of my pants and I move his hands firmly to my ass. His strong fingers squeeze my cheeks hard—there will be bruises in the morning.

I kiss him, sucking his lip, letting go reluctantly.

"And Camas?" he asks, his out of focus eyes fixed on my smeared mouth.

I stiffen and attempt to escape from his lap, but he grabs me, pulling me back to him. I resist. "I don't want a partnership with Camas. Only with you, Beau."

Beau groans. Groping under my shirt, he unhooks my bra with one little flip. He rips my shirt and bra over my head and grasps my breasts. He buries his face, sucks my nipples. Then his tongue probes my throat. He enfolds me in his arms, bucks up against my crotch. Shuddering, he mutters in my ear, "What do we do about Camas, then?"

"'We?' Camas is your problem, Beau."

Beau lifts gray eyes to mine, pleading. "What do I do?"

I raise my arms fast and hard, breaking his grip. Swinging my leg, I dismount and rise to my feet. I challenge him in a parody of his own pose—legs apart, fists on hips, bare-breasted. He sprawls naked and erect on the cushions of the sofa.

"This is what you're going to do, babe." And I give Beau Cassidy my instructions.

Beau is gone. I've brushed my teeth, washed my hands and breasts, and donned my clothing. I write up a précis of what Beau had told me, retrieve the Olaf flash drive from around Sarah's neck, download the story, and put the lanyard back over her head. I dismantle my tablet and destroy the hard drive with a meat tenderizer.

Wearing a pair of Nichole's rubber boots, I cross the yard into the national forest, dig a hole with a garden trowel, and bury the pieces. If Nichole wanted the *Nécessaire* to be kept secret, who am I to share the information with the authorities? Sarah's Olaf flash drive will be detected by her daddy. It's up to Seth Atkinson to determine what to do with my compilation.

I curl up by Sarah, my head on her pillow. She's fast asleep. I am in so much abdominal pain, I can scarcely think. Will I be able to continue with Act II of this tragedy without collapsing? I must for Sarah's sake. I stroke her hair as I watch her sleep. She smells like baby shampoo, innocent and fresh. Is what I'm feeling the love of a parent for a child? How can love be so achingly intense, so wild, so fraught with worry? How do mothers ease into a routine of raising their precious children when the world presents so many dangers? Did my own mom just give up under the pressure and cease to even see me?

Of all the children who could have fallen into my lap, I was so lucky it had been Sarah. Nichole was an extraordinary mother, raising a bright, happy, well-behaved child while her husband saved lives abroad. She'd been a brave woman but she'd made a terrible mistake in confronting Beau Cassidy about the stolen egg. In keeping her father's treasure secure and anonymous—toward what end? Was it worth it?—she'd run into a freak: Beau's girlfriend Deputy Cates.

Unwittingly, Nichole had led her daughter into jeopardy.

Camas Cates masterminded the dumping of the bodies in the cave. She is in possession of the *Nécessaire Egg*. Cassidy is a dick, but a weak and indecisive one. If he had visited Nichole Atkinson without taking Cates with him, what would have been the outcome? He hasn't Cates's iron center, her ruthlessness and drive to dominate. Could Nichole have survived this string of events, even if without her family's legacy?

For a moment I drowse, wondering what might have been if I'd had a family—maybe a daughter like Sarah—and if I'd built a social group of friends and acquaintances and my kids' school friends. But I know that this never could have been— the revulsion I hold toward men runs too deep. Perhaps I could have adopted a child, built a life communing with other single mothers. I sigh. Don't be ridiculous, Olive, you can't even tend to your one 'friend'. I realize I haven't given QC a thought until this moment. Not important.

I leave Sarah in her warm safe nook. I carefully re-do my makeup. I set the scene in the living room: burning candles are dotted about on teak tables and I arrange a bottle of cognac and two snifters on the coffee table. I examine the wood stove, a suspended space capsule enameled bright orange, sleek black flue disappearing into the ceiling. Taking a flock of New Zealand sheepskin rugs from a closet, I array them near the sputnik. I check out the extensive collection of CDs on the shelf. Leonid had loved classical music, Broadway musicals, and movie soundtracks. I'm pleasantly astonished to find the track to *The Usual Suspects* and I slip it into the player. Listening to the lush, almost unbearably melancholy orchestration, violins just stringent enough to set moviegoers' teeth on edge, I remember John Ottman had been both editor and composer, weaving the visual and the aural seamlessly together toward one of the most genius endings in noir film history.

I swig spirits straight out of the bottle. I'm almost out of drugs, maybe it will help. Perched on the unyielding sofa, I allow my imagination to run wild with all the things Cassidy can fuck up, all the scenarios in which everything goes wrong. It's almost 3:00 a.m. when I hear his truck engine burble up the road, across the lawn, and around the back of the house. I'm chilled and stiff in the unheated house and I shake out my arms, trying to relax, to seem welcoming. The music, and remembering the evil genius of Keyser Söze, has psyched me up for this encounter.

Beau shambles in, his frame somehow smaller, defeated. He's dressed in filthy torn jeans and his running shoes are caked with mud. He wears a wrinkled flannel shirt and tee under his unzipped fire department slicker. There is blood splattered liberally across his clothing. He's got a twig caught in his mussed hair and a long scabbed scratch across his forehead. Beau absent-mindedly drops a cardboard box on the table. He slumps by my side.

"It's done?" I ask, soft and soothing.

"It's done."

"Let me see the egg, Beau." He leans forward, unfolds the flaps of the box, and with grimy hands brings out an article loosely wrapped in a blue towel. His fingernails are caked with something dark. As he places it on the table, the towel falls.

The *Nécessaire Egg* is the most beautiful human-made object I've ever seen, the actual three-dimensional sculpture even more exquisite than Faberge's drawing. The gold surface of the egg gleams with an unmistakably

171

authentic luster. The egg is swathed with textured gold rose leaves and petals, so subtly overlapped and interwoven that I am dazzled by the artistry. Ruby and emerald buds nestle into the petals and leaves. The diamond set at the top of the egg is colossal—I can't imagine the carat count. Even in the dim light of the table lamp the complex facets coruscate. I stroke the rose vines twining together to form the tripod base. Tears flood my eyes, that my species could create an artwork so fine. So costly.

I gingerly raise the egg and lay it gently on its side on the towel. I press the cunningly-fashioned jeweled latch and the egg smoothly opens to reveal a tiny forest of gold and diamond handles fitted inside. One by one, I draw the tools out and arrange them beside the egg. All thirteen are here—the treasure is complete. I unscrew the wrought gold stopper of the crystal vial, fantasizing I detect a whiff of the long-deceased Tsarina's perfume.

Beau is watching me. I pull my attention away from the prize, my eyes alight with dreams of riches.

I urge him: "Tell me everything."

Beau rouses himself, pours a measure of cognac into a snifter, and gulps it. "Whoa!" He coughs and clears his throat. When he can speak, he says, "I called Camas."

"Where was she?"

"At home. Florence. I told her that the egg was worth a fortune, mentioned the website you showed me. Asked her to bring the egg and meet me at my place, that you'd contacted me and were demanding $100,000 in exchange for the evidence that we'd killed Mrs. Atkinson."

"Was she upset?"

Beau's exasperated. "Well, yeah, of course. She was furious until I told her you'd discovered the Toyota SUV in the forest using some kind of satellite thingie and had hidden the proof of the theft and death in the vehicle and that you'd tell us exactly where to recover it after the transfer of money into your account. Just like you said she would, Camas said we'd be fools not to check out the Atkinson SUV ourselves before we even considered how to come up with the cash. Said she'd drive her own truck and meet me near the Toyota."

I insinuate my arms around him. He no longer smells of male sweat but stinks, his scent tinged with blood and decay.

I whisper into his ear, "And then what?"

"I waited up there on the logging road. She had farther to travel. Camas drove up and parked. She kissed me hello. I asked about the egg. She said it was in a box on the passenger seat, that she had a brilliant idea about where to hide it. Come on, she said, let's find the evidence. She switched on her flashlight and tugged at my jacket to come with her. We walked up the track toward the Toyota. Camas asked me what I reckoned we were searching for— envelope, flash drive, SD card? I said I didn't know."

Beau pauses, pours and knocks back another drink. I tighten my embrace.

He continues. "I was behind her. I had the cord you gave me and I pulled it tight around her neck quick as can be, but Camas threw her weight back against me and we fell on the ground, her on top. She clawed at the rope, trying to get her fingers under it, but I'm stronger and she couldn't do it.

Beau's breathing is faster now. I murmur, "Great, Beau. Then what?"

"She's kicking the hell out of me—I'm all bruised up, gonna have to avoid the showers at the firehouse. Then she goes to gouge my eyes out." Abrupt silence.

"And?" I prompt.

"And so I broke her neck." Beau is barely audible.

I lay my palm on his cheek, turn his face toward me, gaze directly into his eyes. He's burst a blood vessel in the left one. "Good, " I praise him. "You did everything perfectly, Beau. She was going to blow everything. You see that, don't you?" I kiss him gently and guide his head to my breasts. He nuzzles me as I pick out the twig and leaves from his hair.

"I know," he mumbles.

I stroke his hair. "Did you follow my instructions?"

Beau nods. "Exactly what you said. I drove her truck up and left it by Mrs. Atkinson's Toyota. I stuck Camas into Atkinson's SUV." He takes a deep inhalation, exhales.

"Prove to me that you did what I told you to, Beau."

With difficulty, Beau winnows out a worn reddish shop rag folded into an irregular square from his pocket. He unfolds it, revealing a finger, slim and clean and feminine, the end bloody and ragged, the white ends of the bones visible within.

I stare, fascinated by the token I'd demanded proving Camas's death. I gingerly touch the nail with its pearly polish.

"What did you do it with?" I ask.

"Hunting knife," he mutters. "Blood all over the place."

I modulate my voice, wheedling, "What was it like, Beau? To snap her neck? To cut off her finger?"

Beau peers into the dark as though into the far distance. After a moment, he says, "It was exciting. It was goddamn exciting."

Suddenly, he lunges at me, his mouth hard on mine, his body electrified. He crushes me into the cushions of the sofa. He's heavier and stronger than me and he's hurting me and I'm smothering, fighting for air. He thrusts his hand—that hand with the dark stuff under the fingernails—down my leggings and digs his busy fingers into my vagina.

I tear my mouth from his and shriek, "NO!" I pummel him with my fists and fight with my legs to push away. "This is not how we're doing this, Beau. NO! This is not the way it's supposed to happen." I break free and squirm to the edge of the couch, fall on the floor. On hands and heels, I scrabble backwards from him, furious, panting, struggling not to scream, not to run.

Beau is frozen. "I thought—"

I slowly sit, straighten my legs, grab hold of my fear. Get a grip, Olive.

I soften my expression. "You thought right, Beau." I pout. "But I'm so little and you're so big. It's claustrophobia—I cannot bear to be crushed."

Beau glances at me knowingly. "I get it. You like it on top."

I grace him with a brilliant smile. "That's right, baby. Also, I'm freezing. I've been waiting for you for hours." I rise to my feet—not letting him see how much it hurts—and saunter to the coffee table. I pour him another drink. I let my eyes drift to the sheepskin rugs before the stove. "I need us to be warm, Beau. Light a fire while I change, pretty please?"

Beau drains the cognac and stands, wary. He'd just gotten rid of one crazy woman and now he's stuck with another?

"Where's the wood?" Beau asks.

I fetch the canvas log carrier and Beau takes it from me. But then he drops it on the floor and roughly pulls me close. Kisses me carelessly, caresses my butt, lets me know he's in charge.

I reluctantly disentangle from his embrace with a giggle. "The wood's out on the deck."

As I lead him to the sliding glass door, I step on the bubble wrap, making it crack like whips.

Beau, startled, exclaims, "What the fuck?"

I shove the sheet of bubble wrap aside with my foot. "Insurance in case you brought company," I reassure him.

Sliding the door open, I point at the woodpile by the deck. He strides to the other side and kneels, rapidly piling logs onto the canvas.

I've soundlessly crept after him. I'm on his heels. I lean down and shoot Beau Cassidy in the base of his skull with my pink 9mm. The shot is deafening in the quiet woods. Beau collapses bonelessly to the deck. I thrust the barrel into his chest wall and fire into his heart. I feel for the carotid. He's gone.

I tuck the Nano into the small of my back in the waistband of my leggings. Retrieving the severed finger, I poke it deep into Beau's jeans pocket. From Nichole's bedroom I fetch the coverlet with its brightly-hued geometric print and flip it over him. If Sarah wakes up early it won't do for her to accidently come upon his corpse. I fuss and tug at the fabric, centering it with precision. I pile more and more logs on the edges to secure the coverlet in the wind. I realize I'm violently shaking. The night begins to swirl and tilt around me.

I barely make it to the bathroom, puking into the toilet until I'm empty. Choking, I fight to catch my breath, clenching the stool with shaking hands. I flush and struggle to get up. Steadying myself with a hand flat on the wall, I hobble across the bedroom to care for Sarah.

I silently enter the closet, close the door, and kneel. She is sleeping profoundly, snug and tucked in. I crumple beside her in the cozy den.

Rest a minute, Olive, just rest.

Chapter Nine

Slumped on the floor of Leonid Osipovich's closet, I dully contemplate his old-guy clothes hanging above my head. Nichole had not yet had the opportunity or the inclination to clear the home of her father's things before her fatal run-in with Cates and Cassidy. Cassidy and Cates, sort of like Bonnie and Clyde, outlaw names. Gray dress slacks and khakis hang neatly on the hangers along with ironed shirts. There are nine—I count them—cardigan sweaters in various tones of sludge; clearly, Leonid saved his color sense for the design of his work. The closet smells musty with a faint whiff of cologne and pipe tobacco and feet. Probably Sarah would find this smell soothing but she's still conked out. Maybe she recognizes it in her dreams. I'm happy to wait with her, content to simply be. I'm drained but I don't dare sleep. Misery helps me stay awake as I watch her.

I envision my Sarah lying doped up in the dark, cold dunes next to her dead mother. The wind hissing in the seagrass, grains of blown sand lodging in their eyelids.

Duped by a woman in a deputy's uniform, Nichole had assumed she was dealing with a law enforcement officer with a reasonable moral compass. I'm so angry with Sarah's mother. Why had she called Cassidy and requested that he visit her home? Why hadn't she asked to examine Cates's ID? Didn't Nichole even notice she wasn't wearing a Lincoln County Sheriff's uniform? Cates had kicked Nichole in the head for no apparent reason, a vicious impulse, making a noise like a dropped watermelon. Must have hit the most vulnerable part of the skull for Nichole to die so quickly. The depraved bitch had almost tased Sarah, then my little girl had been restrained by Cassidy in her room, scared out of her wits. Scared out of her voice.

Cates and Cassidy had loaded Nichole into the ambulance. Sarah had tried to convey her story to me. But since she hadn't had a female EMT doll, she'd demonstrated with two males. And, oh god, the Benadryl—Cassidy had most likely drugged Sarah from the same bottle I'd used. Ah, shit. Ah, shit. The tears flow. I've never felt lower, even after being raped for my ninth birthday. I'll never recover from these events and my part in them. It's time for the final act in this drama but I stay with Sarah a bit longer. I need her, and wonder what I'll do without her.

I have my burner cell in my hand but I'm putting off making the call.

I am galvanized by the sharp rat-a-tat of gunfire in the adjoining bedroom. Snapping off the closet lamp, I struggle to my feet. Not shots, I realize, but popped bubble wrap signaling someone has entered the house through the window. I creep blindly from the closet and nudge the door shut, the Beretta pointed straight ahead. Someone rushes at me through the dark, slams into me with the grace of a bulldozer. We crash to the floor. My nose is full of perfume, cloying and exotic. I struggle beneath a body bigger than me, someone pummeling my shoulders and skull with an object—a gun?—and I gather all the strength within me to knock the thing away and tenacious, wiry fingers are wrapped around my throat and I almost lose consciousness as I twist the gun into a sizeable breast, hoarsely wheezing, "Camas! Don't you want to know what happened to Beau?"

In the darkness, I hear her panting openmouthed, her hot breath on my neck. Callously, I punch the barrel between her ribs and am rewarded with a grunt.

"Let me go," I order. The hands abruptly release and she rolls away.

Scootching on my backside to the bedroom door, I reach up and slap the switch. The brilliant light reveals the lanky figure of Camas Cates sprawled on the carpet, chest heaving, arm flung to the side, her right hand bandaged with gauze seeping blood. Her weapon is nowhere in sight, must have slid beneath the bed. I labor upright and lean against the wall. Like Beau, her jeans are torn and muddy, bloodstains bloom on her thigh. But her long hair is brushed and free of debris. A crimson sweater is rucked up under her breasts; if it's bloodstaincd, I can't tell.

181

Cates turns her head, her cagey eyes sweeping me up and down. She's switched-on, intense, violent. "Ah. Olive and her little pink pistol," she mocks.

"Yeah." I hurt too bad for this shit. "My little pink pistol aimed at your nice flat belly. Get up."

She springs easily to her feet. Wonder Woman. Her maimed hand is supported by her left.

"Walk down the hall." She moves lithely through the door.

I follow, turning on the hall light. "You right-handed?" I ask.

"Yep. Otherwise you'd be dead."

Cates saunters into the living room. I study her. She's wearing skintight jeans, the red sweater, and filthy Teva sandals. Her finger and toenails are painted pearl pink. Several of her nails are broken but the visible hand is scrubbed clean. Shiny umber hair falls past her shoulders in perfect waves. She is, indeed, gorgeous, but with the plastic quality of a mannequin: her lips elegantly sculpted, the planes of her face polished quartz, her skin flawless but for a dull purple bruise coming up on her jaw. Her expression is sardonic, one perfect eyebrow cocked. Though she's smiling, her expertly made-up eyes are curiously empty.

She spots the egg on the coffee table. "Ah, there you are my precious," her voice raspy in an accurate impression of Gollum.

"Take off your top."

Cates complies. She's wearing a black sports bra. Ligature marks on her neck are maroon and clearly defined. So that much of Beau's story was true—she'd been strangled with a cord, unsuccessfully as it turned out. Her body is slim, her arm muscles defined. She'd taken the time to brush her hair and reapply makeup after fighting off Beau. After sending him back to me, fresh instructions implanted in his malleable little brain.

I gesture with the gun and Cates rotates. No cell in her pockets. No other weapon unless she has a tiny dart tipped with some untraceable South American tree frog poison in her pocket . . . I come to with a start. I'm getting silly. Having difficulty focusing. This needs to end pretty quickly.

"May I put my sweater on?" she requests politely.

I nod. "Sit." She pulls on the sweater, shakes out her hair, and sinks into the chair Cassidy had occupied. Same *whoof* from the leather. Same pose.

She frowns, gears whirring. "What the fuck were you doing in the closet?"

I am silent.

Her glamorous eyes widen. "The kid is here!" I stare at her steadily.

"Wow." She is admiring. "You've got balls, I'll give you that."

"Me?" I'm incredulous. "You let Beau chop off your trigger finger. What does it take to do something like that?" If I were a sociable hostess, I'd offer her an Oxy.

A spasm of anger crosses her face. "I was out cold after Beau tried to murder me, so I didn't feel him sawing on me with his knife."

"He thought you were dead?"

Cates shrugs. "Yeah. He was sure he'd strangled me but actually he'd pressed the carotid and out I went. I came to after he'd already done it. Hurt like a motherfucker."

"He lied to me about breaking your neck."

"Well, yeah, obviously." Camas smirks at me.

I raise my eyebrows. "Then what? Did you just act like nothing had happened?"

She lets out a mocking laugh. "First of all, I scared the shit out of him. We're lying in a tangle of grass and sticks and rocks up in the forest. I gain consciousness and can't fucking believe how bad my hand aches. I barely have my eyes open. I can see Beau 'cause the flashlight's on the ground. He's on his knees, holding a bloody hunting knife. So all of a sudden I drag in a huge breath and open my eyes wide. Beau scuttles away from me like a crab. It would have been funny but I was too pissed."

"Good times," I say.

She throws me a look. "Then he sort of disintegrated, cried like a baby, swore he was sorry. He confessed to me all about sweet Olive and what you'd forced him do."

"So you kissed and made up?" I'm highly dubious.

Cates is irritated with me. "Think, Olive. I need Beau to take the rap for the death of Nichole Atkinson. I plan to disappear into the sunset with the egg. Of course I kissed and made up. I was full of sympathy for his plight. He bought it. He's not the brightest crayon in the box."

"But he might be the prettiest."

"True."

"And so you sent him to me with your finger in a rag? Beau said you were tough. Don't you want to get it reattached?"

"Yeah, about that, where is it? And where is Beau?"

"He left and took your finger with him. I sent him back to you. Didn't you pass him on the road?"

"No." She eyes me. "Why would I believe you?"

"You don't really have a choice. We're coming up on the deadline. I need to check in with my contact who's ready to release this whole sorry story. Then all hell will break loose. Didn't Beau explain all this?" I'm testy, frustrated with her obtuseness.

"Yeah, but I'm not convinced this data guy exists," Cates scolds, wagging her remaining forefinger at me. "If it's as you say—that this evidence is set to be released to the authorities?—you'll lose all chance at the prize. Beau said you adored the egg, your eyes sparkled at the thought of a thirty-three million dollar pay-off. You are dying to be rich, aren't you, Olive? Stop working at a stupid job? Move someplace warm like Belize?"

I cock my head. "Sure, who doesn't want to be rich? But of course to have thirty-three mill, I need to cash it in all by my lonesome."

"Hey, would ten million bucks be so bad? Split the money three ways? You, me, and Beau, we deliver the egg wherever, divvy up the money, and then we all go our separate ways."

"Why would I share?" I'm honestly curious.

"Because I'll kill you if you don't." Her voice is conversational.

I waggle the Beretta at her.

"You're exhausted," she observes shrewdly. "You have to sleep sooner or later. I'll shoot you. Then I'll kill the kid, too."

"You know, Camas, you really are bonkers."

"You know, Olive, you better believe it."

Standoff.

I watch her. She asks, "Where's Beau?"

"What was the plan, Camas? He was supposed to return here and do what?—in this double-cross of yours."

"We knew you'd have him covered with your silly little pistol. I instructed him what to say and do."

"Did you encourage him to rape me?"

"Didn't have to. He was—how do I describe it?—eager."

"Then what?"

"So while you and Beau were fucking—I assume on your corny fur rugs?" Cates nods at the sheepskins in front of the woodstove, "I would shoot you."

"And after that?"

"It's simple: Beau and I sell the egg."

"Aw, Camas, I don't buy it for a second. What was the *real* plan?"

Camas Cates regards me with the intensity of a great blue heron stalking its prey in the slough. "You'll like this," she assures me. "I'd shoot you with Beau's Glock."

"Then you'd kill him with my Nano?"

She glances at me with approval—I'm an apt pupil. "Fingerprints on the proper weapons, everything perfectly staged. Mutual murder."

"And?"

"I take the egg, go home, and wait for the news to break of Lt. Colonel Atkinson returning from Iraq only to discover the tragic double homicide and theft committed on his wife's property."

"Un-huh. And then?"

"Beau told me all about the article about the egg found at a flea market. I looked it up myself. After mourning my poor murdered boyfriend, I'll eventually travel to England, sell my egg, live like a Tsarina."

"You need the provenance."

"I will make you tell me where it is."

I sigh. "You can try. But I repeat: I've already sent the evidence to my data guy."

Cates sneers at me, "Your imaginary data guy."

"You understand what I do for a living. Why would you doubt me?"

"Because you're a devious cunt," she says, eyes narrowed in hatred.

I smile at her. "Camas, you're so damned smart. But you have one major flaw: you can't imagine how easily Beau is manipulated. He's scared of you, but he *luvvs* me cause I'm cute and cuddly and I admire the hell out of him."

She stills. "What do you mean? Where's Beau," she asks for the third time.

I keep it simple. "You've been triple-crossed. When Beau came back, I persuaded him to tell me everything. Moreover, surprise! I lied. The egg is a copy, a clever reproduction. There is no provenance. It's not worth thirty-three million dollars, maybe a couple thousand."

Cates stiffens, her face blank.

It dawns on me in an instant: I've pushed her too far. Now she's insecure, alone, and in a corner without a weapon. She's got nothing to lose if there is no treasure and no Beau. Cates's weapon is in the master bedroom. All she has to do is retrieve it and she can shoot me and get rid of Sarah. I look at her with sudden uneasiness. She catches my expression.

Cates surges to her feet, snatches up the sharp bejeweled penknife from the array of tools surrounding the *Nécessaire*, and dashes for the hall. I fire as she disappears and the round splinters the corner. Lumbering after her, I fire again and miss. I tackle her just as she grabs the bedroom door knob and we slam to the floor. I clench her legs as she crawls, dragging me with her. Then I feel her tense and her powerful leg drives her foot into my pelvic area. My grip loosens as pain explodes through the middle of my body, radiates up my spine and down my legs.

Cates seizes my left hand and with a vigorous thrust, nails my hand to the wall with the blade of the penknife. Shrieking, agonized, I fire, the bullet shredding her calf, blood bursting and soaking her jeans. She is tougher than I am and doesn't let out a sound, body frozen in pain, bleached skin stretched tight across cheekbones keen as shards of basalt.

"Jesus, Camas, stop," I gasp, panting. I'm curled up in agony, holding my gut, hanging from the blade, dithering between keeping the gun aimed at Cates or dropping it to pull the knife out of the wall.

"Fuck you," she spits, scrabbling toward the bedroom door, striping the cream carpet with a wide ribbon of red.

"Oh, for crissake, this has turned into *Blood Simple*," I mutter. I aim the Nano and shoot Camas Cates in the ear with my last bullet.

My lights go out.

I open my eyes with no sense of how much time has passed. The hall light blazes, the house is silent. Before me, Cates lies crumpled and still. I expect her to leap to her feet, rubbery, adaptable, invincible. But clearly she is dead. I listen apprehensively. Incredible as it seems, Sarah seems to have slept through the gunfire.

189

Hanging from my hand nailed to the wall has resulted in a whole new level of anguish. I fix my eye on the ornate knife impaling my hand, blood drippling in rivulets down the white wall. I feel myself starting to fade out. Rolling slightly onto my side, I brace myself, grab the diamond-studded handle with my right hand, and yank it free. My arm falls. I stifle a shriek by biting my upper arm. I cradle my hand, sobbing, eyes squinched shut. The black fin flits across my eyelids, tempting me toward an end to my suffering.

But I have to care for Sarah. It takes everything I've got to get to my feet and stumble to the bedroom. My working hand is clumsy as I turn the handle and look in at Sarah. Fast asleep. Motionless. Alarmed, I crouch and put my fingers on her pulse. It is strong and steady, her breathing easy. Good. I've saved her from the murderer. Like in *Sling Blade*.

I tightly wrap up my hand with Grandpa Osipovich's silk muffler. In the living room I swallow a slug of cognac. I have yet another corpse to hide from Sarah's eyes. The insurmountable chore looms. How can I accomplish this task? The solution comes to me slowly.

I knot four of Grandpa's neckties together into a rope and bind Cates's ankles with them, pulling the knots tight with my good hand and my teeth. Grasping the end, I drape the silken rope over my shoulder and tow Cates step-by-tortuous-step into the bathroom. Dropping the neckties, I step carefully over her body. I set the latch, exit, and lock the door behind me.

Then I see her long lustrous hair is trailing out from beneath the door and I drop to my knees, attempting to stuff it back with my hand. In vain—the space is too narrow and the hair snarls and it won't. Get. Under. The door.

I am whimpering. I sit back on my heels. Breathe in, breathe out, Olive.

In the kitchen, I dig out a metal spatula from the drawer. Kneeling by the bathroom door, I poke her hair, strand by strand, until it disappears. There! The last evidence of Camas Cates is hidden. I wait in apprehension, certain her locks will slither back out like a litter of baby snakes.

After washing the penknife with soap and water, I dry it carefully, fold it up, and tuck it into the *Nécessaire* along with the other toiletry utensils. I'm trembling badly. I inhale deeply, seeking calm. I've been mauled. There is no part of my body that hasn't been bruised, torn, stretched, or pummeled. I image dark blood pooling in my abdominal cavity, cancer cells spewing into my circulatory system, poison carried to the far extremities of fingers and toes. The torment of extreme pain is keeping me from reaching my goal—I gulp the last three Oxycontin left in the bottle.

I gaze at the golden *Nécessaire* on the coffee table. The richness, the craftsmanship, the jewels and gold—none of this is meaningful. The egg is merely a gilded trinket now, with no particular allure, its long history no longer of any interest. Struggling to my feet, I carry the *Nécessaire Egg* to the study and leave it in its place among the fake eggs.

Wearily, I lift my butt onto a stool at the kitchen counter and paint my pink Nano with the Chanel Liquid Mirror nail enamel I found in Nichole's bathroom. I've had it with people laughing at my gun.

Studying the first faint light on the distant water of the Pacific, I text Lt. Colonel Seth Atkinson and instruct him to come to the house and pick up his daughter.

Chapter Ten

Once again, I wait on the annoyingly angular sofa. Every light in the house is blazing. A restless wind is up, smacking the unlatched front door against the wall of the entry. Outside, night is lifting and the Douglas fir on the other side of the yard gradually reappear. The banging door is nerve-wracking but I'm unable to get up and close it. I'd collapsed here and wrapped my tormented carcass up in a blanket but I'm cold, bone-deep, nothing that can be alleviated by a hot bath or a cheerful fire or a bucketful of barbiturates. Weakness and pain are an eternal part of me now.

I've said goodbye to Sarah, kissed her silky cheek one last time. She sleeps on soundlessly, in deep motionless serenity, the way she does even when she hasn't been drugged. She's oblivious to the danger she's been in, slumbering through the drastic, horrible events taking place in her grandfather's house. I wonder if Sarah's mental snapshot of her mother fallen motionless to the floor of the kitchen is etched permanently in her mind. Will she be tortured by this memory? Perhaps a therapist can help her grapple with her mother's death. In what fashion will she recall her time with me in our various hideouts?

I hope she will not inherit my larcenous streak, after witnessing how easy it is to steal other people's possessions. I yearn for her to remember me with tenderness and forgiveness, if not love. But Sarah's safe, her innocence has been maintained, and her final days with me have been benign. For her sake, I long for forgetfulness, that she retains nothing of this time in her life, that as soon as she sees her father smiling down at her she will begin a new chapter of happiness (albeit without her mommy) and will regain her speech.

Down the road, hounds begin to howl, their eerie ululations echoing in the dawn. A moment later I, too, hear the sirens a long distance away, screaming closer down the Coast Highway, the cacophony growing as multiple vehicles growl up the steep gravel road. Abruptly the sirens cut, leaving a breathless silence. There is a long wait—fifteen minutes or so. I am patient, swaddled in misery, awaiting a denouement. Perhaps a SWAT team is silently creeping up on the dangerous kidnapper holed up in the house, but I can't arouse myself to care.

Movement in the front doorway, a head peeking in and ducking back. From the kitchen comes the sound of bubble wrap popping. A uniformed Lincoln County sheriff's officer wearing a bulletproof vest angles fast through the front door, sweeping both outstretched arms in an arc, a huge formidable-looking gun held in his hands. He creeps carefully forward, eyes fixed on me, followed by a second officer, also armed. The first man is shouting at me. I don't understand what he says, focused as I am on the third figure to enter: Lt. Colonel Seth Atkinson wearing camouflage battledress, his sun-ruddy face intense and angry. Atkinson focuses his blazing blue gaze on me and I meet his eyes. I smile with relief and affection. I am so grateful to him, so glad he is in the country, in this room. He frowns, disconcerted.

Quickly raising the gleaming Beretta from my lap, I straighten my arm, aiming at the group of three. Almost simultaneously the first deputy fires his weapon and the slug smashes me back into the cushions of the sofa and my empty silver Nano clatters to the floor.

I feel an immense weight on my chest. As I lay gasping for breath, I hear, "Sarah! Sarah!". . . running feet on hardwood floors . . . people yelling, even more sirens splitting the quiet dawn.

I will Dr. Atkinson to find the yellow Post-it on the frame of Grandpa Osipovich's open closet door: "Sarah had one Benadryl at 9:00 p.m. after eating a good dinner."

Her daddy's home, Sarah's fine, she's beautiful, she's going to live a long full life. Now she will find her voice.

I fly out into the night sky, circle around Venus, float high above the *Charlie B* struggling across the Great Blue Hole of Belize, trailing forty-foot trains of green gunk fouling her hull . . . Anna Goodreade strains toward me from the stern of the Bremerton ferry, sobbing, beckoning, as the ferry plows the chop of the Sound . . . Nichole sits in a small blue boat caught in a whirlpool of the Siuslaw, slowly spiraling away as

Sarah fights to escape my grip and crawl over the railing of the promenade. I hold her tight.

I am a camera at the bottom of a David Hockney-aqua swimming pool, pointing my lens upward toward Cassidy and Cates, floating face down on the surface, hands entwined, reproving eyes fixed on mine, scarlet ribbons of blood flowing from the stump of Cates's finger . . .

I alight on the sand floor of my cave and there, at last, is the upside-down vee framing that black fin patrolling relentlessly, tirelessly through the moonlight shining on the sea.

ABOUT THE AUTHOR

Mary Frisbee is the author of three mystery e-books: *Satori Ranch*, *Puzzle Creek*, and *Keyhole Spring*; and the textbook *Visual Workouts*. After a career as a professor of drawing, she now concentrates on writing and making art. Artist Mary Frisbee Johnson's work in drawing, metals/jewelry, and sculpture has been exhibited extensively in over one-hundred national and international exhibitions, including twenty-one solo exhibitions; her work is in the collection of the British Museum, London, England. Frisbee lives on the Oregon coast in the small town of Waldport.